RUTHLESS KINGS

A DARK, WHY CHOOSE ROMANCE

BLACK HOLLOW ISLE
BOOK TWO

DANI RENÉ

Hey gorgeous!

I'm dropping by to let you know that with all the changes on Facebook, and notifications being so strange, there's a new community where I'll be sharing a lot more news on upcoming books, sales, and even exclusive stories, including bonus scenes from old favourites! So, head over to Ream, you can FOLLOW for free, or sign up to one of the exclusive tiers.

https://reamstories.com/danirenewrites

See you there!

Light is easy to love. Show me your darkness.

— R. QUEEN

DEDICATION

To my girls who don't follow the rules.

PLAYLIST

Guest Room - Echos
Sacrificial - Rezz, PVRIS
Contaminated - BANKS
Sweat - ZAYN
Hurt You - Living in Fiction
Roses - Awaken I Am
Into It - Chase Atlantic
Love You Like Me - William Singe
Die For You - The Weeknd
Renegade - Aaryan Shah

For the full playlist on Spotify, click here

Please note this is book two and is the conclusion to Judah, Kai, Valen, and Brielle's story. There are some scenes that could be triggering, so please proceed with caution.

PLEASE NOTE: This is a why choose romance, and it includes MM scenes as well.

Life doesn't always bring you what you need when you want it. Fate steps in at times, and it throws shit at you that you least expect. And at that moment, you may think it's the worst thing that could ever have happened to you. Perhaps it is. But you'll never receive anything you can't overcome, or that you can't handle.

We grow from our darkest moments. Like a seedling planted in the depths of the earth, we wait it out. Humans count life in hours, minutes, days. Weeks and months pass, and we live out those instances with abandon. Some reckless, some not.

But each time we grow through the shadows, through whatever pain and challenge we are given, we come out on the other side. We find the light. Even if we didn't see it then.

The darkness of my past has followed me for so long, I didn't think I would ever step out into the light again. But then, I met the two men who changed my life.

I grew up with hatred in my heart. Love wasn't an option. I didn't want to feel those emotions for anyone ever again. Even though I convinced myself I would die alone, it was Kai and Judah who forced me into the light.

They came along and made me see I wasn't wrong. It was those around me who tried to break my spirit. With the actions of others, my soul shattered. And then two men mended it. There may still be cracks, but at least I know who I truly am.

I've come to accept my natural instinct.

I've come to learn that loving someone outside of the social norm isn't wrong, it isn't blasphemous. It doesn't matter what the world says, they only want to force you into their own perceived notion of what *normal* is.

I don't live by those rules or beliefs. And in the future, if I ever have children, they will grow up to learn the same. My story may not be easy to learn, but I know Brielle will soon have to listen to it.

The idea of delving into the past—confessing the memories that haunted me for years as I was growing up—sends revulsion through me. It's difficult. But nothing in life is easy.

The sun is rising on a new day. And I look forward to the ceremonies. Perhaps the darkness that has followed us for so long will pass.

But with Judah and Brielle, and the challenges they face, I'm sure it's going to be a bumpy ride to the light.

THE GUNSHOT that rings in my ears sends both Judah and I to the ground. His heavy weight on top of me, keeping me pressed into the soft grass. The scent of earth invades my nostrils, but the fragrance of his cologne—spice and warmth—takes over and soon, all I can feel, hear, or smell, is him. It's as if he's burrowing himself in my veins. He's the blood that's coursing through me, keeping my heart pumping, keeping my lungs filled.

"Get the fuck off me," I bite out as I push away from the lawn, but he's too heavy, too strong.

"Remember when I told you that you'd never escape me, that if I found out you're a lying little spy, I will end you," he reminds me, and I still all movement. The frozen state of me makes him chuckle. The vibration of his chest against my back sends rage racing through every nerve in my body.

He's right though. He told me that, and I didn't listen. I should have come clean, but I was scared. My father didn't tell me all he wanted from me. There was no conversation between us about his plan. Overthrowing one Boss is difficult, but trying to overthrow three, that's another story altogether.

I should never have listened to him. In the past, Papa had radical plans to free us completely from the ties to Italy. I believed him. When I was younger, he painted these beautiful stories about how we'd never have to live a life within the confines of an organisation, even though ours was one of the more infamous. But it wasn't because my father was a hero, it was because he broke the most important rule within our world.

More shots ring out, but then there are some that come from the house, and I hear it—death. Lifting my head as much as I can, I glance out at the perimeter of the estate, but I can't see anyone from where we are.

"All clear." A few of the soldiers who work for Judah come sauntering past as they shoulder their weapons and head indoors. Suddenly, I'm left shivering on the ground as Judah stands, and offers me a hand. I don't expect him to help me up, and I don't know why he's doing it, but I gratefully accept.

He tugs me to my feet before gripping my face between his thumb and forefinger. His eyes are dark, filled with rage and malice.

"Such a pretty little spy," he hisses in a low, sadistic tone. "Too bad you're going to have to pay for Daddy's sins." There is no denying I've fucked up, but he wouldn't kill me. Surely not. "Take her to the dungeons." He shoves me away from him just as Kai steps out onto the lawn.

I stumble into the arms of that man I've come to learn is so broken, so tortured, I wanted to save him. But looking up into his dark stare, I realise the person who cared for me is no longer present. In his place is a stranger.

"Judah, please listen to me," I plead as I'm pulled in the opposite direction. "Please," I beg once more, but the man who I'm meant to be marrying in a few days is no longer paying attention to me.

Yes, I have made a mistake, but it's not what he thinks it is, at least, I'm sure it's not. The email from my father told me one thing, that he's going to free me and end the reign of the Veniers. But he didn't tell me how. All I had to do was to lure Judah outside, which I didn't do, but instead, he forced me into the garden.

"Kai, please, if you just listen to me, I can fix this." My words, though, they fall on deaf ears because as much as I would like to explain myself, none of these men will hear me. When I see Valen, I meet his frosty glare, and I pray he'll be the one to actually take on board what I need to say. "Val, there are things that are out of my control. You have to talk to—"

"Time for talking is over, princess," Valen says to me and I'm shocked at how hostile his tone is with me. I've never seen him like this, not with me at least. "You'll have your time to state your case, but right now is not it."

Kai drags me behind him and I'm tempted to fight him off, but even if I did, there is nowhere to run. There are no escape routes for me because every man on this estate will have now been told about my double-crossing.

"Like father, like daughter," Kai whispers as we reach the cold underground dungeons. And I'm shoved into the same room where they held me hostage for a few hours not that long ago.

I didn't think I'd ever be here again. And yet, I find myself in darkness. I don't fight, I don't scream. My father did this to me. He's the one who put me here. Anger bubbles up inside me and it's about to erupt. All my life I saw him as a hero. I looked up to him, and I believed in the stories he told me.

It was my naivety that forced me here. I should have questioned more. There were no facts that my father gave, but he convinced me he was the good guy. And what daughter would discount her father's testimony?

I jump when my cell phone vibrates in my pocket. I forgot it was there, and I think Judah didn't realise I had it on me. When I pull the device out and glance at the screen, I want to scream. My father's number glares back at me. It's a message, one I don't want to open, but one I know I have to read.

078 543 56980: I'm sorry, my sweet pea. I'll come to you. Just wait and do nothing rash. There are things at play you're not privy to, and when I can, I'll explain.

I DON'T BOTHER RESPONDING BECAUSE MY ANGER HAS taken a hold and I don't believe or trust anything my father tells me. I don't delete the message, I leave it in the inbox and lie back on the cold, hard mattress.

In the dark, the screen is blinding, as I open the

message Judah sent me weeks ago. It's the photo he tried to distract me with when I was training with Kai. Things have certainly changed. Granted, he still wanted to kill me, only now, he had a reason to.

When I first arrived in Black Hollow, I was a pawn in a game, and now I'm the losing piece on the board. I didn't know my father's entire plan. He kept all the important information to himself. I only learned about the diabolical idea last night.

My thumbs hover over the screen as I look at Judah's photo. He's on his bed, the mirror across from him reflecting his shirtless body. I can't deny, even now, I'm attracted to the arsehole. There isn't any sane reason for me to be, but there's an underlying lust-fuelled current that races through me every time he's near.

I go back and open a new message before scrolling down to Valen's name. He's been my friend since I arrived, and I am hoping I can get through to him even if it means I'm about to lose my phone. Once they realise I have access to the device, it will be removed from me and I'll be left alone in the dark once more. But I have to try.

I promised myself before I got on the flight to Black Hollow I would never stop fighting, and I don't intend to do so now.

. . .

ME: VALEN, I KNOW YOU WILL LISTEN TO ME. I DIDN'T know what was going to happen until last night. Please talk to Judah, make him listen because I never wanted to hurt any of you.

BEFORE I CAN SAY ANYTHING MORE, I HIT SEND AND leave it at that. I don't want to tell them I love them. Not yet. This is the time to focus on getting out of this fucking dungeon. It's so cold, I shiver the moment I lie back and allow my body to relax. There are so many things racing through my mind. And I'm pretty sure the one and only thought that makes sense is Judah will no doubt kill me. If he does, the blood will be on my father's hands.

The soft vibration of my phone sends me into a mild panic. But then I see it's Valen. I don't want to open the message, because I'm scared he's going to tell me he hates me. Deep down, I can live with Judah hating me because I don't think he ever cared for me, but I had found a friendship with Val, and for him to turn his back on me would hurt far too much.

. . .

VALEN: THERE IS NOTHING I CAN DO NOW, PRINCESS. You're in the hands of Judah. We may all own you, but he's still the one that's going to marry you.

IT WASN'T WHAT I WAS EXPECTING, BUT AT LEAST HE hasn't told me I'm going to die. They're all angry, and I don't blame them. But when I have my moment to speak, I'll explain what happened. The email from my father only told me enough to force me to obey, but I had a choice.

And if given the same fork in the road, I know which way I'll go. They have used me as a bargaining chip for the last time. I will not be played with, or played, ever again.

I curl into a ball, bringing my knees to my chest, and I allow my eyes to flutter closed. I'm exhausted. There has been too much to think about, and as darkness steals me, a memory filters into my dreams, reminding me of why I wanted to leave London.

I DON'T ENJOY BEING HERE, BUT I HAVE NO CHOICE SINCE Papa is at work. When he told me I should be friends with Marco, I thought nothing of it. He was merely a boy from what I can remember of my childhood.

"Buttercup," Marco calls me by the nickname he's given me. "I think we should go for a drive. Perhaps we can find a quiet place away from the house." He reaches for my face, trailing his knuckles over my cheek. It's almost as if he's taking in a piece of art, but his eyes hold malice that sends ice racing down my spine.

I'm not sure why he wants to leave, since my father isn't home. But I don't feel at ease with him anymore. Something shifted between us last night when he tried to kiss me and I pushed him away. He didn't like rejection, and I didn't like him.

"I'm not in the mood to go out," I tell him as I pull away. We have snogged before, and there were times I enjoyed it. He's not a bad-looking guy. But he doesn't set my soul on fire, he doesn't make my skin burn at his touch. That's what I want, what I've always craved. Perhaps I'm reading far too many romance novels.

"I think you should listen to me, darling," Marco coos, but there's no gentle tone to his voice, instead, it's drenched in a darkness that makes my chest tighten and my stomach recoil.

"Perhaps you should leave. I'm sure you can find someone to join you on your escapades." When I meet his dark, stony stare, I can't help but shiver. He's no longer the friendly young man my father brought to the house. Over the months, he's changed, and I know my initial *gut feeling about him is true. He's not a good person at all.*

"Make no mistake, Brielle," he whispers as he leans in close. His lips brush along my cheek, sending revulsion coursing through me. "I'll be back. I don't like being sent away like a child, but for now, I'll respect your decision."

That's when I feel the cold metal grazing along my neck, and a gasp of shock races through me. The sharp blade kisses my flesh, and I know if I were to move just an inch, I'd be bleeding all over the steel.

"Enjoy your night, Brielle," Marco murmurs in my ear once more. "I'll be watching." And then he turns to leave. When I hear the front door shut, I sag into the chair and let out a breath I'd been holding as I met his angry stare.

I'LL BE WATCHING.

The words force me to sit up in the darkness and I can't deny, I'm shaken. I know I killed Marco, but he had allies. A man like that never walked the city alone, and when he called on the men who followed him, they obeyed. He may not have been a Boss, or even Underboss, but as a well respected Capo, he brought about a wave of obedience in the men.

They didn't want for anything because Marco made sure they got what they asked for. And in return, they got their hands dirty when it came to the schemes he planned.

The creak of a door echoes in the dark, and I push to my feet. They're coming for me, and I have to be ready. This time, I'm going to have to fight for my life. Judah will not allow me to kill anyone else. He will not want to test my loyalty. He's going to want to kill me if I don't offer what I know.

And even then, I'm not sure he'll let me live because I betrayed him. He knew what was coming before I could tell him. Before I could warn any of them, Judah was already privy to the plan. Which means he's been spying on me. I suppose it puts us at even levels when it comes to lies. However, my future husband will not see it that way.

It was my father who forced his hand. It was my bloodline who started the war that's just started amongst our families. And there's not much I can do to stop it now.

Question is—*Will Judah still want to marry me? And if he does, will he ever forgive me?*

WE'RE GOING to be the Ruthless Kings soon. It's a name that will be given to us when we step up to the thrones of our families. I thought I would have a queen beside me, but she lied. She hid things from me I can never forgive. And now, I will walk on this journey with Valen and Kai.

I don't love her.

I felt nothing for her.

That's the same mantra I tell myself every single fucking day.

But I know it's all a lie.

When the door slides open and scrapes along the concrete ground, I don't wince, but I do grit my teeth. I hate the sound because it reminds me of what my father used to do. When he brought me down here, he wanted to teach me what we, as Venier Bosses, needed to do. He enjoyed it. There was never a time I didn't see satisfaction on his face when he walked into this dungeon to torture, maim, and kill someone.

Granted, I was convinced I'm the same as him. Throughout my life, I wanted to be, and as much as I enjoy the job, I don't do it to innocent people. My father had no morals. Even though I live a violent, chaotic life, and I have most of the students in this school, on this island afraid of me, it's nothing compared to what the old man was capable of and it makes me wonder if Jordan will become just like him.

Brielle stands in the darkness. Even cast in the shadows, she's beautiful. I know Kai and Valen feel the same. I can practically *feel* them vibrated with the need to make her pay. But this torture isn't like the others we've dished out on disloyal subjects.

There is something vastly different about what we're about to do. We conversed and agreed. Kai wanted to take the lead, but Valen stepped up. He's been her friend since she arrived, which makes sense he should be the one to dole out the first round of punishments on our pretty little spy.

Val steps forward causing Brielle to step back.

But when he crooks his finger, it's as if she's mesmerised by him and obeys. It's an erotically exquisite sight to behold.

"It's time," he tells her and I allow him to move past both myself and Kai toward a room we haven't used in years. I've only ever seen it in action twice before. Once by my father's hand, and the second by my own.

Marco's filthy whore he sent into my home to spy on me and the guys was dealt with in the only way we know how, by making her beg.

And Brielle will meet the same fate. The only difference is, she's going to have to survive all three of us. And that's definitely not going to be easy. The corner of my mouth quirks into a grin as we follow Valen and Brielle.

"Don't enjoy this too much," Kai whispers. "Someone might think you're in love with her."

I snap my glare to his, and he knows he's walking on thin fucking ice in saying that. But then again, my best friends have known me most of my life, and they can read me like a book.

I haven't allowed myself to say it or consider it. But I can't deny it's an emotion that's slammed into me a few times since laying my eyes on her.

But I'll fight it.

I can't love a liar.

I can't want a spy.

And I certainly will break her before she becomes my queen because even though I hate my father's last wishes, I'll never go against them.

The room we take her to was designed for something other than the violent torture we usually dole out. It's been locked up tight for so long, I'm expecting it to be a mess, but I'm surprised when I find the tools shiny and shimmering.

"What the fuck is this?" Brielle snaps when her gaze lands on the large, wooden St Andrew's cross which sits against one wall. It may look like a dungeon of a talented Master, but it's far from it. Instead, it's here for amusement.

We've not really used it for its true purpose. And perhaps Brielle will be our first.

"It's time for you to tell us everything," I say as Valen and Kai take the lead and bind her wrists to either side of the large X. Once her ankles are secured with the soft, leather cuffs, I can't help but smile.

"I told you everything," Brielle argues, her voice tight with annoyance. I'm surprised she's not fighting us. Her gentle obedience is rather intoxicating, but it can't be real. Her father's email was clear to her—she's infiltrating our home, sending him details that should never be known to anyone outside these walls.

"You see," I start without looking at her. I keep my eyes on the table which is filled with implements to either bring pleasure or pain, depending on how they're used.

And if I were honest with myself, I'm not entirely sure which I'd like to dole out on this pretty princess just yet.

Lifting my stare to hers, I smile. "I don't believe you."

"I don't give a shit at what you believe or not." Her fire is back, and it makes my dick hard. What I would like to do right now is to make her take my cock all the way down. I'd love to feel that slender throat constrict around my shaft, and I want to make her swallow every fucking drop of my seed. And when I'm done, I'd love to watch Kai and Valen take their turn with our pretty little toy.

I pick up the long, sleek blade that's lying on the table, and I make my way toward Brielle. Kai is at my right, while Valen is at my left. The three of us stand silently taking in Brielle's now trembling body.

"Are you going to be honest with us?" Valen says, his voice is void of any emotion. Even though he's been the one to befriend her first, he's realised that she lied to us. She's hidden things we needed to know. Anger at my father for choosing her for my wife takes a hold of me.

"I only got that email last night," Brielle insists, and even though I know that's not a lie, there are things she's still keeping from us. There is no doubt in my mind she's got more intel about her precious father.

I take a step closer before I lean in and run my nose along the soft, smooth flesh of her cheek. She smells of fucking salvation and lust. Brielle is a contradiction, beautiful, yet so utterly dangerous.

"You know something, little spy," I whisper in her ear. "I think I'll let Kai handle this." Even though I know watching one of my best friends torture her perfect body will make sure I'm rock fucking solid, and my cock will ache for release, I'll also enjoy hearing her beg.

When Kai steps up toward her, he tugs the knife from his belt holster and allows the tip of metal to kiss her cheek gently, before running it down toward her neck.

The movement is so slow, so meticulous, and the tremble that shakes through Brielle is rather beautiful. There is a threat behind his movement as he presses ever so slightly into the delicate flesh, but I can tell he's restraining himself from his white knuckle grip on the handle.

When he reaches the neckline of her top, he allows the sharp edge to slice through the material, and it gives way easily. Once the cut is made, he holsters the knife and uses his hands to rip apart the delicate cloth, and underneath we're gifted with her breasts cupped in black lace.

But we lose Kai to the task because his knife comes out once more, and he drops to his knees. This could be mistaken for a scene of lust and desire, but it's filled with violence and anger.

"Please, Kai," Brielle begs, and I'm not sure if she's turned on or afraid, perhaps a bit of both. "Please, I promise you I'm telling the truth." A mingling of emotions coursing through her like a tornado. A storm about to wreck the pretty princess. She's a deceitful liar, a spy for her father.

Anger surges through me and I lift the leather crop in my hand and grip the handle so tight, I can feel the imprint of the pattern burrowing into the flesh.

When Brielle is left in nothing but her underwear, I smile when her gaze lands on mine.

"Judah," she whispers my name, a broken word on her tongue, filled with emotion. "Please."

"You've lied to us before, when you didn't tell us you knew Marco. That you were dating the prick," I tell her, reminding her of her omission. "And the moment you received the email from your father, you also decided it was easier to hide it."

"I wanted to tell you, but it was too late. You knew, and you didn't want to listen. You were the one who took me outside."

"Because I wanted him to see what his daughter had become," I spit as I make my way toward her. Stopping inches from her trembling body, I allow the leather to lick against her skin. I don't miss the way her breath catches when it slides along her nipple.

"And what exactly is that," Brielle spits, anger taking over the fear, and I can't deny, I'm hard as rock. My cock throbbing against my zipper as I look down at her.

"You're ours," I tell her, even though the idea doesn't sit well with me. "And you wanted this, you chose to stay even when we told you the truth about our relationship."

"And that's why I'm still here. I'm not fighting you, Judah," she spits angrily as she pins me with a glare. It's cute that she thinks she can make me cower with her angry stare.

I lift the leather crop and bring it down onto her nipples earning me a gasp of surprise. While Kai rises to full height beside me, he leans in to run his nose along her neck, up to her cheek, and I watch as his teeth graze along her earlobe, sending more waves of shivers through her.

"But you still lied," he whispers, loud enough for all of us to hear him.

Valen comes toward us, stopping behind me. I may feel the burn of her lies, but he befriended her when Kai and I held back. I didn't trust her, while Val tried to argue that she was a good girl.

Val's hand snakes up her stomach, between her breasts, and his fingers reach for her neck and they wrap around the column perfectly. There are no words between them, but the anger coming from both of them is palpable.

"You're going to do something for us now," he tells her. "To make up for all that you've hidden, all that you've tried to keep from us."

"I'll make this right," Brielle chokes out and I tease the leather against her stomach, trailing it down between her spread thighs. Her heated gaze locks on mine, while Valen's hand is still gripping her throat.

"You're right," Kai says as he rests the blade against her sternum. We're all three overwhelming her. She's distracted by the desire, by the fear, and by the need to fix what she broke.

I may not love her, but I'm still going to marry her. Even though I'm tempted to kill her and send parts of her back to her father, bit by bit. I'm going to make him pay for trying to kill us, to kill the soon to be Kings.

What he doesn't realise is that his precious princess will be *our* Queen.

I lift the crop and bring it down on her pussy, causing her to gasp once more. The sound is beautiful in the dungeon's darkness. I repeat the action over and over again, while Valen tightens his hold on her neck. The struggle in her gaze is obvious, and as she tugs at her restraints, she looks from me to Valen, to Kai. But neither of us aid her. Instead, the torture continues. She's so close to the edge when I stop my ministrations, and Valen releases her from his hold.

We step back, take in our princess as she pulls in a much needed breath. "You're monsters." Her voice is ragged, but I can't help smiling at the way she still fights back, even though we could so easily end her life.

"Hate us all you want, princess," I tell her. "You're still a possession in this house. You were born a bargaining chip in a war that was started by your father."

"Bargaining chip or a weapon?" Brielle throws back easily, fire dancing in her eyes as she looks at us.

Kai takes two long strides and stops inches from Brielle. "If you want to be a weapon," he hisses in her ear. "You'll be *our* weapon. Is that clear?"

Brielle's gaze flickers to mine as if she's looking for help. Perhaps she wants mercy. I don't know what that word means. But I can read the realisation in her expression. There is a shift in her demeanour because she comprehends her situation. As I tip my head to the side to watch her, she will not die today.

She looks back toward Kai. "What do you want me to do?"

"You're ours," Kai says, and leans in close. "And that means you will obey our orders. Because we're about to send you to the front line of a war, your father started."

Valen takes a step toward her, stopping to her left, while Kai leans in to her right. But it's Val who continues, "You're going to be *our* little spy," he tells her, the corner of his mouth tipping upward. "And you'll betray the one man who used you all your life."

"You want me to go undercover with a man who taught me everything I know?" Brielle laughs. It's a humourless, bitter sound that makes her come across as more ruthless than I expected. "He'll see right through me. He knows when I'm lying, and—"

"We know when you're lying," I interrupt her little tirade. "I knew the moment you walked into this house that I couldn't trust you, and here we are."

"I can't do it."

"Oh," I say as I stop in front of her. "But you can. Because tonight, we're going to a party, hosted by one of the most dangerous men in Italy, and when we do, you'll be beside me, as my soon to be bride. And you'll be the one who will find out all the information we require. Think of it as…"

"A test," Valen finishes my sentence. "It's a challenge for us to make sure you're loyal to the right side, to the men who will without a doubt, end your life without a second thought."

There is a darkness, a rigid anger in his tone. He will not forgive her anytime soon. I've known Valen for far too long, and I know when he's hurt. Brielle has most definitely gotten under his skin.

She looks at him for a long, heavy moment, the silence is filled with guilt and regret coming from her. "Fine," she finally whispers. "I'll do it." Her eyes turn glassy as the tears sit on her lashes, waiting to fall.

"Of course you will," I tell her. "Because if you don't, I'll make you watch as I gut your father like the lying bastard he is."

I spin on my heel, but can't help the smile that curls my lips when I hear her gasp in shock. The thing is, I'm going to kill the fucker, anyway. She just doesn't know it yet.

BROKEN TRUST

VALEN

I SHOULDN'T BE angry with her, but I am. I've spent a lot of time with Brielle since she arrived at Black Hollow. Out of the three of us, it was best for me to take the lead, to ease her into this world. Only because I'm the least threatening.

Judah is an unfeeling bastard when he wants to be, and Kai, well, he's the fighter of the three of us. And he looks like he could easily snap her neck.

Kai doesn't let up as he glares at her. Even though Judah has just walked off, heading for the liquor cabinet I'm sure, she's still under Kai's ruthless stare.

"I don't like that you're a liar, and I don't trust you'll do what is needed," he informs her. "But make no mistake, I will end you. I'll enjoy watching this pretty, silken flesh bleed." His threat is combined with the gentle touch of his fingertips as he trails them over her collarbone.

"I won't betray you," Brielle whispers, but Kai isn't listening. His hand cups one of her breasts, and I watch with need coursing through me as he pinches her nipple harshly, causing her to cry out in agony. "Please, Kai. I promise you."

I can't deny watching her beg for mercy has my dick hard as stone. Her body trembling as Kai lifts the leather crop that Judah was using over her nipples. They've hardened to tiny peaks, and my mouth waters to have a taste. To know how delicious she is.

"I wanted to tell you about the email. I've said this repeatedly. I can't repeat myself if you're not going to listen." Her voice is strained as she glares at Kai. Even in her predicament, she's still as fiery as the moment she stepped off the plane.

"You'll get mercy," Kai finally says. His words clearly surprise her because she snaps her gaze to mine before looking back toward Kai. "If you can prove you're loyal to us only. Tonight, little mouse, I will be your shadow."

I take a few steps back, allowing Kai his moment. Because soon enough, it will be me who will need to bathe her, and get her ready for this fucking ball. I hate black tie events. They're the bane of my existence, but I have a feeling this one will be very different to all the ones in the past.

"I answered Judah's request. I'll do as you all ask and get the information you need. There is no need for this anymore," Brielle snaps as she tugs on her restraints. She's going to be bruised if she continues, but I can't bring myself to stop her. The anger and heartache from her lies are still fresh in my mind.

"She's all yours," Kai says with a chuckle. He hands me the crop and heads up to the house. The darkness of the dungeons cloys at my vision. I hate being down here, especially for long periods of time.

"Valen," Brielle whispers my name, it's a plea on her lips as she looks at me with those pretty fucking eyes. I can't bring myself to *want* to hurt her, not when she's staring at me as if I were her saviour.

Before she can say anything more, there are footsteps behind us, and I'm pretty sure I know who it is from the laugh that's coming from the stairwell.

Jordan walks into the room where I'm setting all the tools away. Brielle is still bound, in just her underwear which has been cut from her body. But I don't move to cover her up.

"Well, fuck me," Jordan says as he moves deeper

into the room. "No wonder my brother is losing his mind over the princess."

"I think if you don't want your brother to gut you, you'll keep your gaze averted," I warn him. Even though he knows about our relationship, the connection between the three of us—Kai, myself, and Judah—Jordan never talks about it.

"Just looking," Jordan says with a chuckle and holds his hands up in surrender. "Listen, are you all flying out tonight?"

"Why?" I close the drawers on the metal cabinets that house the more dangerous tools before turning my attention on the younger Venier.

"I wanted to invite some friends over."

I stop what I'm doing and arch a brow at Jordan. He's only a few years younger than us, and I have a feeling he's going to be worse than Judah ever was. There's mischief in his eyes, darker, more malevolent than his brother is. Or was.

"Does Jude know?"

Jordan chuckles. "No. But I don't think he'll mind. He's on a call and I can't find Kai. I'll have everyone gone before you get back."

"Mmm," I mumble. "Yeah, we're all flying out in a couple of hours. Remember though," I tell him. "Nobody goes into the offices."

"I know, I know," Jordan says, but his gaze still flicks toward Brielle who I know is still bound, helpless, and she can't do anything to change her predicament.

I make my way toward her and undo the cuffs. First her ankles, then her wrists. When I try to check them for bruises, Brielle pulls away from me, the anger in her gaze palpable.

"I'm fine."

"Oh, the princess is not happy with you," Jordan taunts, and I pin him with a glare from over my shoulder. "Here you go, sweetheart." Jordan shrugs out of the jacket he's wearing and hands it to her. And the gentleness she regards him with twists at my heart. Picking up the clothes that Kai sliced from her body, I offer her my hand which she doesn't accept, and I allow it to fall at my side. She's as angry as I am.

"You better be ready tomorrow," I tell him as I lead Brielle from the dimly lit room. "Judah wants to meet with all of us."

We have to discuss the events that will take place soon. As we all step up into our roles as Boss of our respective families, Jordan will take over from where Judah is now. There is no escaping where we're all coming from or where we're going.

"I was born ready," Jordan informs us with a confidence that makes me smile. As much as I find him a mischievous little shit, he's a good kid.

"I can walk on my own," Brielle murmurs as she tugs away from me, and I allow her the space. We did little to her, less than we could have done, but I know Kai wants to test her tonight. "What is this party for, anyway?"

"It's a dinner," I tell her. "All the Underbosses who are soon to be taking over their respective organisations will be in attendance."

"So there'll be other women there too?" I'm not sure if it's hope, or fear in her voice, but there's a hint of something.

Keeping my gaze averted, I don't look at Brielle, because I can feel her stare on me. I turn and make my way up the steps, and listen to her follow right behind.

When we finally reach the main floor of the house, I take her hand, even though she tries to pull away, and I lead her up to her room.

"You don't have to be nice to me," Brielle says, her voice breaking on the last two words. "I know you hate me, and I don't blame you, but I need you to believe I would never do anything to hurt any of you."

Coming to a stop inside her room, I turn to regard her. "I don't have to believe you because you haven't given me a reason to. I'm just here to get you ready for tonight." I release my hold on her hand and make my way to the wardrobe. The moment I pull both doors open, I'm met with an array of designer dresses, all in her size.

"I'm not a doll that needs to be dressed," she bites out, her anger clearly taking over, and it makes me laugh.

"I know," I say without looking at her. "But for this event, you need to look…" I'm not sure how to phrase it to not freak her out. The women who will be in attendance tonight are all there because they were forced to be. Brielle is mostly going of her own free will. It's new.

But, the dress code for any females within the company of the up-and-coming Bosses, needs to look like arm candy. As much as she'll hate it, she'll also have to accept it.

"I need to look like what, Valen?"

Her hand landing on my shoulder stills me for a moment before I pull out a hanger from the closet. The long, sleek black dress has thin straps, simple design, and the slit that will land at her left hip, and will go all the way down to the floor.

"I'm not wearing that."

"You can and you will," I tell her as I glance at her from over my shoulder. "Go shower, freshen up, and put some make-up on." The order doesn't beg for debate, but Brielle opens her mouth. "Now."

We have to leave soon, and I'm not in the mood to deal with Judah and his frustrated sighs if we're both late.

"You're angry," Brielle finally says, her voice softer now. "I get it. And I'm sorry you are. I should never have kept anything from you."

I perch the hanger on the handle of the door before I turn to her. "No," I say, "you shouldn't have, but the past is just that, and we can't change it. For now, you'll find your footing by listening to us, and obeying our commands."

Even as I say it, I'm unsure of what tonight will bring. There are men who will be in attendance, watching over all of us.

"And you get me out of it," she says. "What do I get?"

The corner of my mouth kicks upward into a smirk. Lifting my gaze to hers, I answer, "You get to live."

"So you'd stand by and watch Judah kill me?" There's a challenge in the question. One that I don't want to get into, but I have no choice because Brielle will push more and more until I've succumbed to her needs. And fuck, I so badly want to bend her over right now and make her scream my name. But that would make her think I have forgiven her.

I take measured steps toward her. When I stop inches from where she's standing, I hold my hand out. "Jordan's jacket," I say. "You don't want Judah to see you wearing that."

For a moment, I'm sure she's going to challenge me, but then she relents and shrugs out of the heavy material. I take the item before I turn and head for the door.

"Will you be ready in twenty minutes?" I look over my shoulder, my eyes on hers as I watch the annoyance dance in her eyes and the frustration written all over her face.

"Yes," is the only word she utters before she disappears into her attached bathroom. She has everything she needs in there, so I leave her be. It's a lot to take in when you first arrive at Black Hollow. And even though Brielle has been here for a couple of months now, we've not made it easy. Or, I should rephrase, Judah hasn't made it easy for her.

Not that I blame him. Not anymore.

When I reach my bedroom, I find Judah leaning

against the closed door, arms crossed. He's in a black tuxedo with a crisp white shirt. The uniform that's worn to all these dinners and events.

"Is she ready?"

"She will be," I tell him.

He pushes away from the door, taking a step toward me as he leans in close. "Don't let her get to you. Out of the three of us, you're the one who will more than likely break first."

I chuckle as I press my lips to his ear. "Want to see her break? Let's see if she'll play a game. Truly test her," I whisper.

Judah puts some distance between us, the surprise on his face is clear. There is one thing that takes place at these events most of the women hate. It's part of becoming welcomed into the family.

It's easier to kill than to go through the test.

"She'll be angry if we test her like that, and I have a feeling that exposing her to others won't sit well with me. I don't share with bastards like those," Judah says finally, with a nod. Deep down, I didn't expect him to agree. "I'll be out in the car."

Once I'm alone, I head into my room to get ready for the evening ahead. I've been to these every year since I turned five. When I was little, it would be the most exciting night of the year. We would be allowed to sit amongst the elders. All the Bosses would talk about business. And even though we didn't truly understand what they were talking about, not really, there was a sense of importance which came with being a part of it all.

It doesn't take me long to get ready, and I'm tense as I make my way down the stairs. I'm not sure what Brielle is going to do, but as the three of us wait for her, all dressed in our tuxes. I know that the moment she descends those stairs, we're going to be more than fucking distracted.

A TEST OF LOYALTY

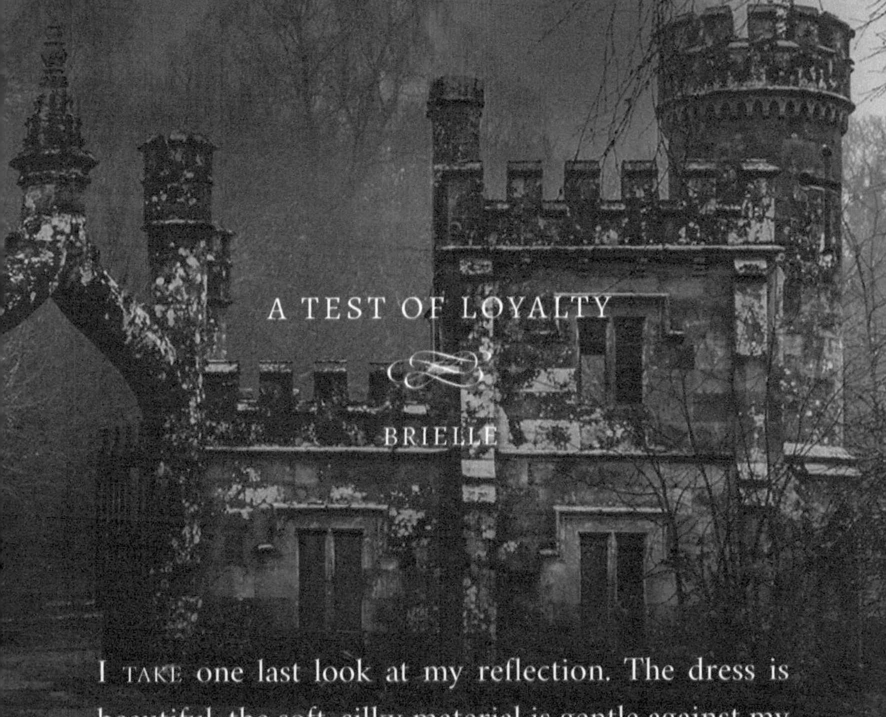

BRIELLE

I TAKE one last look at my reflection. The dress is beautiful, the soft, silky material is gentle against my skin. I made my face up with dark eyeliner that accentuates the colour, and my lips are glossy. I've added a dark shadow to my eyelids, giving off a smoky effect. And I've left my hair loose. The sleek, silken strands hang to the middle of my back. A dark curtain in case I need to hide.

I'm unsure of what to expect from this event. Growing up away from this life, I've not gotten used to gatherings like the guys have, and I have a feeling they will not be as protective of me as they would have been if they didn't learn about my father's plan. When I think about the man who is meant to look after me, the man who raised me, I can't stop the anger from taking over. All I ever did was look up to him. I thought he was a hero. I still haven't gone through the folder Judah gave me on my father.

Once we're back from this stupid party, I'll have to do it. Instead of putting it off, I should learn who he really is. I hope there's also information about my surgery. I quickly take my medication before I grab my purse and head out of the safety of my bedroom.

The house is silent as the low lights illuminate the old gothic building in a soft yellow glow. If it wasn't so eerie, it would be beautiful. There is a heaviness in the air, malevolence that fills the home reminding me it's not a normal place to live. There are dangerous people who inhabit it. Men who will kill me if tonight doesn't go well.

I know why they're doing it. This life is one where you have to prove your loyalty. And I have to do it, or I'll never see my next birthday.

When I reach the top of the stairs, I find the front door ajar, and I can hear their voices. I'm not sure if Judah is outside smoking, but they're all on the porch, waiting on me. My stomach flips, twists, and my heart rate spikes as I take the steps one at a time.

The slow descent feels as if I'm walking into a

gauntlet. I'm about to be pushed outside my limits. I'm sure of it because they will not take it easy on me.

When I finally get to the door, I pull it open to find three of the most beautiful men I've ever seen on the other side. They're all in black tuxedos. The sharp contrast of the black and white makes their olive skin even more prominent. Breathtaking.

I wanted so badly to hate them. Even after they took me down into the dungeon earlier, I forced myself to be angry, but I couldn't. I should have come away worse off than I did. Even though they'll never admit it, I'm certain they showed mercy.

"I'm ready," I finally say since nobody else is speaking.

Three sets of eyes take me in. I'm nothing more than a pawn once again. This time, it's of my father's doing. Kai hands me a thin, elastic holster which has a small loop added.

"Put this around your thigh, and make sure you're able to grab this," he says as he hands me a small knife which has a handle made of what looks like shimmering porcelain. There are thin marbled lines of gold through the white. The blade is small, but it can do damage, like he taught me.

They don't avert their gaze when I obey him and slip the black band around my thigh, pulling it high. The slit of my dress goes all the way to my hip, so the weapon will be visible, but as long as I'm able to grab it, I don't care.

"Am I really going to need this?" I ask as I look at each man dubiously. Even though I've killed before, I don't want to make it a habit to be walking around with a weapon on me.

"I have no doubt," Judah says, a smirk curling his lips as he regards me before turning and heading for the waiting car.

Kai walks behind me, while Valen is in front of me. I'm led to the vehicle, like a lamb to the slaughter. That's how it feels, anyway.

Once I slip into the seat, I'm cocooned by Kai and Valen. The driver starts the engine, and soon enough, we're on our way to the airstrip. The flight isn't long, and I know that in a matter of hours, we'll be on the mainland. After that, I'm not sure what's going to happen. More so, I'm not sure I'm ready for what is about to happen.

"Tonight, you'll listen, you'll obey, and you'll answer only when spoken to. Am I understood?" Judah's voice holds authority, more so than it has before.

"Yes," I answer with a nod.

"And if you're offered a drink, you accept," Kai says. "The men will want to see if you're able to hold your own."

"Am I going to be put on some parade there?" I bite out in frustration as my stomach somersaults at the idea of being watched. These are soon to be Bosses, they're not going to be friendly, and they certainly won't be kind.

"You, along with the rest of the women, will be tested many times throughout the evening," Valen tells me, his tone softer than it was in the bedroom earlier. "You will need to pass, because if you don't..."

He doesn't need to finish the sentence because I know what's about to befall me if I fail. There's a heavy silence in the car now, I feel it right down to my bones. I didn't expect them to talk to me, but I can't deny the deafening quiet makes me anxious.

Judah's gaze lands on mine for a moment before he trails that hardened glare over me. From the top of my head, he peruses every inch of me until the heat of his stare makes me tremble.

I can't tell if he hates me or desires me. Perhaps a bit of both. I shift in my seat at the memory of the three of them taking over me. Their hands on my skin, their lips teasing and tasting. I'd never been with more than one man, and yet, the three alpha males that are currently overbearingly angry with me, have my heart. I didn't tell them that, I don't want them to know, not yet.

Hate had filled my heart when I first arrived. Living here wasn't something I had chosen, but something that had been thrust upon me. And unwillingly, I caved in and allowed my feelings to take over.

Perhaps I wanted to heal them, to fix those broken parts I found of each man. I know you can never change someone. But you can love them enough till they feel as if they're no longer shattered.

Deep down, I want nothing more than for them to forgive me. If I hadn't let my guard down, I would never have found the peace I had within the Venier mansion. Even though Judah still frightens me somewhat, I know he's a good person because I can see from the way he loves Valen and Kai. He may act as if he's a cold-hearted bastard, and for the most part, I would agree with that. However, he has a softer spot for the two men.

We finally pull up to the airstrip and I'm trembling. Valen opens the car door and exits the vehicle before turning to offer me his hand. I'm surprised by the gesture, but I accept it gratefully. I didn't think he would be so friendly, especially after everything that had happened earlier today. My mind is still racing with the memory of being bound and at their mercy.

I know they went easy on me, which makes me wonder just how bad it can get if they didn't. We make our way in utter silence to the plane which is ready and waiting to whisk us to the mainland.

Once inside, each of us settle in our seats. This time, I'm not alone with Judah, or Valen. The presence of all three of them in this small space is overwhelming.

"You'll walk in on my arm," Judah speaks after a few moments, capturing my attention. "Val and Kai will be around, watching. If anyone tries anything, you have your blade. However, you will need to remember these are men who have been in this world since they were babies. They do not *feel* anything, they only act. There is no permission asked, so make sure to stay close."

I stare in shock at Judah. I know from my father's stories these men are dangerous and violent. But the idea of being alone with one of them, someone who wants to hurt me makes me shiver. "What if someone tries to hurt me?"

"You hurt them back," Kai says with a grin and it's the first time in a long while that he's smiled at me. "But remember, they take names, they never forget."

"So I can defend myself, but I'll always have to look over my shoulder," I bite out as I roll my eyes at the stupidity of this world we live in.

"And watch that pretty little mouth, princess," Valen whispers as he leans in close. The heat of his breath fanning across my cheek. "They won't think twice about using it."

I snap my glare at Valen, my mouth popping open in surprise at what he's talking about. I'm not stupid when it comes to men and their desires. But I don't for a second believe that the three of them would stand back and watch anything like that happen to me. "And you'd let that happen?" My voice comes out in a sharp, fearful breath when I ask the question.

He grins, before he gestures with his head toward Judah. "It's not up to me tonight. You're his," he says as he looks at my soon to be husband. "And none of the men there tonight give a shit. They'll risk their lives to enjoy any female in attendance."

"That's…" I don't know what to say because if I wasn't afraid before, I am now.

"That's the way of our organisations, princess," Valen says as we take off. It will be a couple of hours, but in that time, I know my stomach is only going to be in knots by the time we disembark. And when we walk into the venue for tonight's proceedings, I'm going to be a mess. Even though I know I have the three of them with me, I can't deny my anxiety is going to be through the roof.

"I'm going to the bedroom," I announce as I make my way to the back of the plane. Sitting on the bed, I take deep breaths, hoping to calm myself. My chest is tight when I consider what's about to happen.

When the door opens, Kai walks in. He's the last person I expected to be here, but he settles in the armchair that overlooks the bed. The distance between us is obvious. It's clear he will not come closer. And deep down, it stings because all I need is some reassurance.

"There are things about this world you're going to have to get used to, and this is one of those times." He leans forward, his elbows on his knees. Those eyes that have always seemed to hide so many secrets now hold mine hostage. "You're a strong woman, Brielle," Kai tells me. "I've watched you fight, train, and spew your fire at Judah for months now."

"That's different."

"Yeah, it's different, but it's still you. If you allow

your mind to play tricks on you, then you won't get through this." There's a deeper warning in his tone. As if there's more to what's going to happen tonight than just a dinner and some expensive drinks.

"And what gauntlet am I going to be running exactly?" I challenge as I cross my arms over my chest. He's right, I am strong, especially when anger and frustration take over.

"Now," Kai says as he pushes to his feet, "If I told you that, it would take away from the fun. Wouldn't it?" He offers me a wink before leaving me to mull over everything in my mind.

I was brought up as a strong person. My father didn't sugar-coat anything when it came to this life. Yes, he held back truths that I should have known about, including the secret about my surgery, but he ensured I wasn't in the dark about where he came from.

The life of a man who has joined the mafia, who swore loyalty to an organisation, is not something to take lightly. And inadvertently, I don't think Father realised that when he sent me to life at Black Hollow, I've now sworn my allegiance. Only, it's just not to the people he wanted me to offer my support.

I lie back and look up at the ceiling. My focus on

the soft cream colour of the light shade. The bulb is dimly lit, only offering a weak, yellow glow.

Judah, Kai, and Valen were right. I came here a shy, scared girl, and I've changed. Over the past few weeks, I've gotten to know them, and I've also learned who I am. My father forced this on me, and he wanted me to become part of a war I wasn't fighting.

He started it, and now, I'm the one who needs to finish it. Father won't be happy with me, and I know the disappointment he'll show will probably break my heart, but he was the one who lied.

As much as I wish it didn't have to be this way, there is no other choice. I'm to marry Judah, and if there's one thing I know, it is that my loyalty has to lie with my new family.

But, I have a feeling there are so many more secrets to uncover. It's not going to be an easy ride, and I don't expect it to be. All I can do is take it as it comes.

The plane slowly descends as we reach the mainland. My stomach drops with every movement of the large aircraft. The nervous energy causes butterflies to come alive in my belly. It's as if I'm going to a party where I'll be the main spectacle. I don't like the focus on me, I never have.

Only this time, I'm not going as just another teenager who's out with her boyfriend. I'll be walking in there as the future Queen of the Venier family. And I'm not sure just how ready I am to claim that name in public just yet.

THE CAR TAKING us to the mansion set on the mainland in Sicily is driven by one man from the family we're visiting. It's only when I saw the crest on the licence plate of the car did I realise who they were.

The *de Rossi* clan is infamous in America with their Boss, Enzo, taking over after his father's death. I don't expect he'll be here, since he lives in New York, which has me wondering about the rest of the family.

"Respect the host," Judah says to me as we come to a stop at the entrance of the property. The car stills before the driver pulls up the long, winding driveway. Dim lighting offers a glow, making everything outside the car seem eerie. It's as if we're coming up to an old castle where Dracula could hide in the shadows. Something tells me there's a more dangerous man who lives in the house that I come to see as we wind around the enormous fountain.

"And who is the host?" I whisper as I look out the window and up at the three-story building to my left. The door opens before Judah can reply, and when the driver helps me out, he offers a small smile before raking his gaze over me.

Judah is right behind me, his hard, muscular body flush against my curves. He leans his chin on my shoulder, and whispers in my ear, "Since you already know of de Rossi, you should know his right-hand man is Mario Errani."

A gasp of realisation falls from my lips. "He's Kai's brother?"

"For the most part, yes. Mario's family adopted Kai when he was younger," Judah explains and I nod because Kai has already told me the story. When he admitted his past, that's when the barrier between us fell, and I knew we had taken a step toward something new. We formed a connection that night, and now I can't believe he's angry with me to the point of not even wanting me near him.

He's kept his distance all day. Even on the flight, he sat the farthest away from me. I meet his gaze for a moment, but he turns away and heads to the door.

"Come," Judah orders before offering me his arm. From the outside, people looking in may think it's rather romantic that we're walking in together, but I know different. "Mario is the one who will lead the dinner, but make no mistake, any of these men here can do what they please."

"What if Mario doesn't like it?"

Judah shrugs, I can feel the movement against my arm. "He'll kill them." He says it so nonchalantly, it's as if he's talking about the weather. To them, murder, torture, and violence is second nature. So it doesn't surprise me when he says, "Or he'll make a public spectacle of them. Mario is happy working for Enzo, even though he'll still oversee a lot of the Errani family business, he has stepped aside to allow Kai to take over. They'll work in unison."

That shocks me. It's unheard of for there to be two heirs, and one to take a back seat to his own family's organisation. "That's never been done before."

We step inside before we can continue our conversation. The house is nothing like the Venier mansion. The exterior is one colour rather than brickwork. And as Judah leads me inside, I take in the modern interior. There are bright artworks hanging on the walls, while the large chandelier takes over the entrance hall.

"There is more to Mario than meets the eye," Judah says once we're greeted by servers with silver trays of champagne, and before he can continue, we're led into the living room which has no furniture except for a long bar along the one wall. The rest of the room has been emptied and I'm guessing it's making space for the hoards of men in black suits and white shirts.

It's as if they've all been given a specific uniform. One they cannot stray from. There are other women. I seek them out with glimpses around the room and find some of them are watching us.

"You're going to be the belle of the ball," Judah whispers in my ear. "I think you may need to watch your back."

"Why? Because you're such a catch?" I throw back my response, and I have to fight my smile when I feel the tension in Judah's arm.

"Don't push me tonight, little spy," Judah warns in a low whisper. "Let's get a drink."

"Venier," a deep baritone comes from behind us, and when we turn, I see a man who looks like he should be on the cover of a fashion magazine.

"Errani," Judah says as he holds his hand out and they shake on it. "This is my fiancée, Brielle."

"So this is the princess on the isle," Mario remarks with a grin. He takes my hand before bringing it up to his lips and presses a kiss to my knuckles.

"It's nice to meet you," I offer with a shy smile.

"I can see why my brother is so intrigued by you," he says then, and my mouth pops open. "He's mentioned he was training you in some fighting. It's good for a woman who is stepping up into a role like you will be."

"He's taught me a lot." I nod, remembering that nobody else knows about our connection.

"Good." He offers me a bow, before he says he needs to work the room. He's an intriguing character, and I wonder if he's also adopted, or if his bloodline was of the Errani clan.

I don't ask Judah. Instead, I focus back on the men in the room. Each of them offers me a quick glance, but when they realise I'm with Judah, they turn away, as if they're trying *not* to stare.

I don't know exactly what the dynamic is between the Underbosses, but I do know there are families who are stronger than others.

We stop at the floor-to-ceiling windows and patio doors that lead out to a back garden. There isn't beautiful greenery, instead, there's a swimming pool that's lit with soft blue lights. The water is crystal clear, and I'm pretty sure if the sun was still shining, it would illuminate the water.

I want nothing more than to run. I want to escape to the island, back to the Venier mansion. Never did I think I would ever *want* to go back there.

But now, being here, I want to go *home*.

I sip my drink, my mind still on the outdoors, and I wonder just how easy it would be to get off the property. Escape hasn't been on my mind for months, but right now, in this moment, it's at the forefront.

The clink of a champagne flute captures my attention, and I turn to find Mario at the fireplace. His expression is neutral, but his gaze is on me.

"Welcome to the Errani home," Mario says with a bright smile on his face. He's handsome, I can't deny it. "Tonight is about getting to know those in this world. Some of you"—he pauses for a moment before continuing—"may already know those in the room. But there is more to tonight than meets the eye. In the coming months, families will work together, form alliances. Perhaps your fathers may have set about rules, agreements, contracts, but this is up to you now."

There's a heavy silence in the room as I take in the faces who are turned to Mario. Eyes focused on the man making the speech.

"We communicate, we plan, and we live our lives within this myriad of agreements, rules, and promises. However, for now, those things will be put on the back burner. It's time to enjoy our dinner."

We're led through the living room into a much larger space with a long, ornate table that's set for the guests. Candelabras are lit, the dancing flames causing the wine glasses to shimmer. As we each take our seats, I'm beside Judah, with Valen to my left, and Kai opposite me. His gaze never strays, even when his brother speaks.

"And dinner is served," Mario announces, and the servers enter, carrying three plates each. They're smaller, beautifully presented appetiser plates. They topped the bruschetta with fresh herbs, small roasted cherry tomatoes, and a drizzle of olive oil.

Even though I'm starving, my stomach churning with anxiety makes it difficult to eat. I have to force myself to enjoy the food. The conversation around the room continues, laughing and chatter, fades into the background as the main course is served.

I take in each of the faces around the table. Most of them are strangers to me, I only recognise a handful. The women who accompany some of the Underbosses are exquisitely dressed. They're poised, ready for a life of servitude when it comes to the men in their lives.

I want to say I'm not like them. But deep down, I realise I would do anything to ensure the safety of Judah, Kai, and Valen. Perhaps it's the guilt of what my father wanted me to do, or maybe it's because I am really falling in love with them.

As dinner ends, we're once more escorted from one room to another. This space reminds me of an open-plan art gallery. The walls are light, while the art pops with bright colours. Only a handful of the canvasses are classics, the rest are all modern art.

A young man saunters up to Judah and I as we enter the room. I don't know him, but the way he's watching me makes me think he knows exactly who I am. Although, most here would know me because of my family name. I'm sure the families in attendance are aware of my father and his traitorous actions.

"So, this is the Saviatti princess," the young man says. He looks like he should be on a runway. His brown hair is short, buzzed close to his head, while his green eyes shimmer as he looks at me.

"This is Brielle." Judah's tone is tight with tension, and his hand finds the curve of my back, his fingertips trace down my spine sending warmth coursing through me. He may be angry at me, but it's a show of possession.

"Well, I hope for Judah's sake you're nothing like your father," the stranger jokes as he glances between me and Judah.

"I'm nothing like my father." My words drip venom as I glare at the stranger before me. I don't give a shit who he is, and I certainly am not afraid. Granted, I should be. He could seek revenge on me for speaking out, for being *rude*.

"Let me make something clear, Dario," Judah says as he steps forward, leaving me two steps behind. The warmth of bodies surrounds me, and I realise I'm now flanked by Kai and Valen. Judah continues, "You can come at me all you like, because Brielle will be a Venier soon. And if you'd like to start a war, I'll gladly fucking finish it for you." His threat is nothing more than a hiss, nobody else can hear it, but I feel eyes on us.

The noise around the room lowers to a soft simmer, and there is no doubt everyone has noticed the altercation between the two men.

Once again, when I didn't want attention, it's found me and I'm left with trembling hands and a wildly thudding pulse.

"Hey man," Dario says as he holds his hands up and chuckles. "I was just testing."

"I don't like you," Judah informs the man before him. "And if you so much as try to *test* me again, I'll ensure you're very sorry you did."

Judah's shoulders are rigid as he glares down at the other man. There's a few inches of difference in their height, and Dario seems to shrink back at the enormity of what's going on between them.

"Everything alright here?" Mario steps up to the circle that's now surrounding us. His gaze is nothing like Kai's as he looks between me, Judah, and Dario.

"It's all good, Brother," Kai responds, because I'm sure Judah is nowhere near calm enough to reply.

Mario nods. "Good," he says. "Wouldn't want something to happen at our event. We should form alliances, not break them down."

Once again, the rules are set without voicing them fully.

"It's all good," Dario says, before he offers Judah a mock salute and turns and heads back to his friends. The tension in the room settles, and I'm able to breathe again.

"I need the restroom," I whisper, hoping to escape the eyes currently focused on me. Without waiting on the guys, I head out of the large room which reminds me of a holiday villa, and make my way down the passage.

There are so many doors leading off the long pathway, and my curiosity gets the better of me as I push one door open. Inside is a darkened bedroom. The only light comes in from the window, illuminating the frame of the four-poster bed.

When I take a step back, I slam into a hard, muscled frame. A gasp tumbles from my lips and a hand slams over my mouth. His warm breath fans over my cheek when Kai whispers, "Shh, little spy."

He steals me from the darkness and pulls me into a corner where nobody could see if they walked by. I messed up by replying to Dario when I should have been quiet. And Kai will not let this go. I can feel Judah's presence not far away, and when Kai spins me around, Judah's eyes land on mine, and then Valen appears like a fucking shadow.

Three Kings too young for their roles, but far too confident in the violence and mayhem.

Kai pulls me back against his body, while Judah and Valen step forward. I'm nestled between them, three men who look like they're about to devour me whole.

"You're going to go upstairs. There's a bedroom to your left as soon as you get onto the landing," Kai instructs me in a whisper. "Bring us the information that's on the desk that's at the window which overlooks the backyard. Two folders with the Errani family crest on them."

"How do you—?"

"Don't forget, little spy," Judah whispers, "don't get caught, and don't fuck this up because it's your chance to prove your loyalty."

Kai's hand tangles in my hair and he tugs my head back, while Judah and Valen both lean in and I feel the warmth of their mouths against the curve of my neck.

Teeth graze my flesh sending tingles through me and my body prickles with goosebumps as I'm tormented. I can't deny, their threatening demeanour has my thighs squeezing together.

"Now go, little spy," comes Judah's order. "Find us in the living room when you're done."

I'm not sure why Kai doesn't ask Mario for them, but I don't question my task. Instead, I rush for the stairs, and make my way into the silent darkness that awaits.

My heart thunders in my ears, and I pray I'm not caught.

BROTHER'S PROMISE

WHEN I FIND Mario in the office on the ground floor, I shut the door behind me and take in my brother. I was adopted, while he grew up with his parents. The thing is, he's never made me feel as if I'm an outsider. And for him to step back and allow me to take over his bloodline heritage means more to me than I ever expected.

"It's nice to see you outside of New York," I tell him as I settle in the chair opposite his desk.

"Enzo said I can take some time to sort this shit out here and get you ready for the initiation. It's only a few weeks and you'll be taking over from Dad."

"I know," I say as I rest my ankle on the opposite knee. "I'm worried though. I mean, I should not be the one taking over. You should."

Mario settles into his chair and he looks at me like I've lost my mind. "You realize that I'm not coming back to Italy. I'm happy where I am. Enzo is good to me and I have to stay loyal. I made my vow already." His New Yorker accent is thick, so far removed from my Italian one.

We both grew up in Sicily, until Mario left to find something better in America, and it left me at home. I didn't mind it because things were good. The house was warm when it needed to be, and it was cool when summer hit. And I had parents who supported me right until I wanted to come to Black Hollow. They weren't happy, but they didn't stop me.

"He wasn't over the moon that I wanted to study here," I tell Mario as I recall our father's words. *It's not a good place. What if you fall in with the wrong crowd?*

"You know the man would do anything for you. It's even in his last will and testament that you're taking over the organization."

Sighing, I nod, knowing that he's right. I shouldn't feel like I do, but I think it's because I was the adopted son, not the blood relation. It makes things a little more difficult.

"I've spent my life fighting this war inside me. I

didn't want to think the way I do, but being adopted changes your outlook."

The thing about it is, Mario and his parents, our parents, never once made me feel as if I wasn't part of the family. It's my own issues I need to deal with. And I have to do it soon because in a few weeks, I'm going to have to take the vows.

"You know you're being an asshole," Mario throws out. "And don't you dare think I'm insulting you. Brothers are meant to spar with each other."

This makes me chuckle. "Oh, yeah, don't I know it. There was never a dull moment in the house growing up." It's a reminder that all my doubts are nothing more than my mind playing tricks on me. I should know this by now. I'm old enough to realise it, but there are times I question everything.

"Is your girl getting everything she needs?" Mario questions. Brielle believes it's a genuine test, where Mario is in on it. I asked him to ensure the folders were ready for her the moment I knew he was hosting the party. It made things a lot easier for us to have her come here and snoop around the mansion.

"Yeah, thanks for doing this," I tell him. "With Saviatti trying to take us out, we want to make sure he knows he can't fuck with us."

"What is the plan once you find him?" Mario

questions as he watches me with intrigue. I have a feeling my brother is going to offer his help.

"I'm not sure. Judah wants him dead, but Brielle has questions. She needs answers, along with her half-brother, Emilio."

Mario's brows lift in surprise. "Her half-brother?"

I nod. "We didn't realise until Judah met with Brielle's dad, and he confessed to being Emilio's biological father. It's a fucking shit show at the moment with the crossing of bloodlines that's been going on. There are also questions about the fact that Emilio's younger sister was killed."

"Are you telling me that Saviatti had her killed?" Mario leans forward now, showing more interest than he was earlier when I was being a worrisome arsehole.

"Well, Brielle had surgery when she was younger, it seems as if the donor came out of nowhere, as if by magic." I recall the admission she told us when we found her medical records. It certainly was a shock to all of us. I didn't expect it. Even when I was training her, she's strong, fast, and her endurance is brilliant for someone who had her surgery.

"Fuck." Mario's response mimics ours when we found out. There is still so much to unpack. There are still secrets hidden under layers of fear. Mainly from Emilio Saviatti, Senior.

"It's been an eye-opening few months, I'll tell you that."

"Are you still…?" Mario looks at me, the curiosity is clear in his eyes. He's the only one outside of the three who knows about my inclinations. And I was honest with him about my love for Valen and Jude. I didn't hide it from him, and then he told me of his own bisexual nature. It was astounding to me because he never ever hinted it. But then again, neither did I when we were growing up. It's only when I got older, I knew Mario had seen me with a boy from school. Nothing happened, but there was a quick slip of the wrist.

It was before Jude or Valen became the only men I will have sex with.

"We have come to an agreement, of sorts," I tack on. "It's the three of us, and Brielle. She knows. There was no way we couldn't tell her, so now that she's been accepted into the family, we're going to try to live our lives free from the judgement of others, but we will have to keep a lot under wraps."

Mario nods then because he knows how these things can blow up. It's difficult when you're in a heterosexual relationship, but add in another person, and there's drama that follows with every step of the way.

"I promise you, Kai, your secret is safe with me. It always will be and it always has been. I can't imagine putting you in any danger, or having a threat on your life because of who you love."

I know he's not lying. We were trained so well to watch for tells. Mario has known my secret, and he's kept it safe all these years. I'm lucky enough to have the support from someone who I've looked up to. When I was younger, I wondered what life would be like if I were to ever have fended for myself. If the Erranis didn't adopt me. I know I wouldn't still be here. Not with the road I was on.

"I better get back to the party," I tell him as I recall Judah was planning on testing the allegiance of our girl.

"I'll be out there shortly."

I leave Mario to work, and I make my way back to the main area of the house where the guests are still gathered. Most of them are not even more drunk than before. I don't partake in the alcohol on offer because I'm alert. This isn't a friendly get together, there are threats in this room. And they would stop at nothing to try their luck.

I find Jude and Val, and I hang beside them to wait until we see Brielle enter the room once more.

"Mario doing okay?" Valen asks me as he glances at me from over his shoulder.

"He is." I keep my watchful gaze on the door, and when I see her coming down the sweeping staircase, I tug at Jude's jacket, and we head out into the entrance hall.

She's carrying a couple of folders, they're not as big as we thought, which makes it easier to carry. I take them and head out to the car to store them before anyone can ask questions.

Upon my return, there's an altercation, and I almost step in, but Valen holds me back when he grips my arm. "Wait."

Judah is having a stare off with some arsehole I've never seen before. I'm not sure if he's only just come up the ranks, but he looks like he's about to get Judah's bad side. You do not want that.

"She's just filthy scum, like her father," the young man sneers as he looks at Brielle. She looks visibly shaken, and every instinct in my body wants to go to her and save her. I know Valen is feeling much the same, but if we do, it may look strange.

Judah is the one marrying here, and he needs to stand up and protect her. "Oh, and you'd like to know if she's willing to do anything to become one of the wives of your friends?" Jude's voice is pure ice.

"I bet she would. Why do you think she's with you? Unless she has some magical cunt that makes her so irresistible."

My blood burns through my veins. I've known anger before, but this rage that's currently coursing inside me, swirling like a fucking volcano, is about to erupt.

Judah takes one step forward, towering over the little shit. He keeps his composure, more so than I would. "Her *cunt*," he enunciates the word elegantly, and methodically. "Is not something you will ever get to experience. Because she is my fucking princess, and she will be my fucking queen. Am I understood?"

I watch Jude, his hands fisting at his sides. I'm not sure what the next step is here. He's clearly laid claim, but I don't see this bastard backing down.

"Why not show us then?" The challenge is set between them. I doubt Jude will do it, but I've seen worse things happen at these parties.

Suddenly, he grips Brielle at the back of the neck, and he pulls her against him. His front to her back. And I watch as his left hand snakes under the slit of her dress. Valen chose the outfit well.

"You want to watch me punish her for being the daughter of a lying bastard?" Judah throws back the challenge. The corner of his mouth tilts when his hand stops. I'm pretty sure he's found our little princess wet.

"Do it." The bastard smirks.

I'd love to know his name. Because I'm dying to get him in the ring with me. A good fight is what I need right now. It would be a welcome distraction from the sight of Brielle being manhandled by Judah. If it were any of these other cunts, I would kill them, but because I know Jude is in love with her, I know she's safe.

As much as our anger had overtaken us earlier with her, we have feelings for the girl. There is no denying she's come into our lives and made them better. I don't know what I would do without her here.

"I'm not one to share my toys. And I certainly don't whip my cock out for just anyone. Or did you want to see it because you'd like to compare sizes, little boy?" Judah taunts the stranger. "But, as you can see," he continues as his one hand wraps around her throat, and the other is still knuckle deep in her underwear, if she's wearing any, "She is mine." And then Judah pulls his fingers from between Brielle's thighs and brings them to her mouth.

Dutifully, she sucks the digits. Two of them slide over her tongue, and Judah pushes deeper, until they can hear the soft gagging sounds of our girl throughout the room.

"She is not a free use toy for any of you," Judah continues. "Every inch of this body," he says as he gestures from her head to her feet. "Belongs to me, to savour, to punish, and to worship. Because unlike you, she's paid her penance."

"I have no penance to pay."

"Oh?" Judah releases Brielle and pushes her behind him as he takes one more step toward the rogue bastard. Then he grips him by the collar, and he drags him until their noses are almost touching.

I'm shocked when he lifts his wet fingers, and he runs them under the bastard's nose, and he smirks. "Smell that? That's the fragrance of a woman, something you will probably never know. Now, get the fuck out of my face, and behave like a man, not a teenage boy wanting to compare dick sizes. Because you know nothing about her, me, or my fucking family. But if you'd like to learn, I'll gladly show you."

I've never been more turned on by Judah before. The show of confidence, the alpha male grit that's currently emanating from him, has me wanting to spend the night fucking worshipping him.

"Fuck me," Valen whispers beside me. "I think we may need to leave this little charade earlier than planned. Because I am pretty sure tonight will be a long, exhausting evening."

I chuckle quietly. "It's like you're reading my mind."

We have been in many situations where we had to step up, to come face-to-face with some challenging bastard, but this was rather exquisite.

Judah shoves the man backward, and he stumbles into his friends who catch him. "Did I make myself clear?" Judah's tone is pure venom.

The youngster has the audacity to laugh, but he does nod. "Yeah, perfectly."

The music starts up once more, and moments later, it's like the stand-off didn't happen. People continue drinking, laughing, and talking. Judah and Brielle join us, and I'm still staring at him, surprised at the show, but turned on like never before.

Valen is the first one to speak because I'm still speechless when I look at Judah. "That was rather interesting."

"Did you have to do that to me?" Brielle asks as she looks at Judah.

He chuckles. The way his eyes crinkle at the corners makes him seem almost happy. It's not every day this bastard smiles. But when he does, it can be a vision to be held.

"Yes." He looks at Brielle, then at me. "I'm not sure who he is, but we should get his name. When we're back tomorrow, I'd like to send him a little gift."

"I'd like to get him in the ring. Although, I'd like to make him cry," I tell Judah. "Fucking little shit will pay for that show of overconfidence. I don't like him."

"I'll find out who he is," Valen announces, and makes his way into the crowd. With his charm, I have no doubt Val will more than likely have a list of names for us—the arsehole and his friends.

"I think we should leave soon before more shit hits the fan," I tell Judah. "We'll wait for Valen and then hit the road. I've spoken with Mario, so we don't have to stay.

"Sounds good. I'm ready to call it a day, and night." Judah's distracted by his phone for a moment, and then he glances at me. "Meeting tomorrow morning early."

My brows furrow in confusion. "Something serious?"

He shakes his head and says, "No, but we do need to meet. A few things on the agenda. And I want us all present."

I know there are a lot of tasks coming up, so I nod and as we wait for Valen, I wonder if we'll have any more threats in the coming weeks leading up to our initiation ceremonies.

WILL YOU FALL?

JUDAH

These fucking *feelings*.

I don't like knowing that she's in danger. But she has to prove herself. The team sitting at the table watches me as Brielle settles beside me. Our lives will become intertwined. But it's not only our personal relationship, it's one that includes the organisation. We're going to be working together. I may be the first Boss to include a woman in the clan, but with the fire I see in Brielle's personality, I know she'll never sit back and let me run things alone.

A queen who will step up to the plate. One who will burn the world down to save those she loves. Which begs the question which is running through my mind on an endless loop—*Will she ever love me?*

The countdown to the wedding is now on. A

couple of days to go and I'll be her husband. I'm going to have to accept the fact that she's my wife, and she will be a part of the family.

In the past, my ancestors never allowed their wives into the organisation. There were never moments of acceptance to have women in this life. Not even at the school. It was only recently that it had come to pass.

I don't have any issues with having women working in the organisations, but they have to prove loyalty. The Agency can deal with them. I, personally, do not hurt women. But if they fuck over the family, they will pay.

"Brielle has taken the first few steps in becoming a part of the organisation," I say as I look at Jordan, then Emilio, Kai, and Valen. The rest of the soldiers sit quietly as they watch us.

Kai leans forward to look around the table before he speaks. "The folders have given us a lot of insight into what my brother found. He didn't want me to get involved in this war that's started, but we need to take steps to protect ourselves."

I believe Mario would look out for Kai. It's something that makes me respect him because I would do the same for Jordan. I would do the same for any of the men in my life.

"It's Saviatti who started this, we just kill him and it's over," one of the soldiers, Giorgio, says then and I understand his reluctance and his need to avenge what's going on.

"We need to play this intelligently. If we rush in with guns blazing, we could lose men. I don't believe in losing anyone in this organisation." My voice is calm, collected, and just a tad cold, but I don't care. My men know me, and they understand that if they don't agree, they're welcome to leave.

"What are the orders?" Marcello asks with a sadistic grin. He's one of the men who will shoot and kill and make me proud. The bastard was an orphan who came to the island wanting to learn and become a soldier. I've known him for years. Even though we didn't build a deeper friendship, I trust him.

"I want Saviatti's team taken out," I say as I lean back in my chair. There is a lot to do, but I want Brielle's father for myself. "If you find him, bring him in alive. There are questions he needs to answer, and I'll be the one who gets the answers."

"What if someone has answers about his whereabouts?" Sergio speaks up as he looks between me, Kai, and Valen. He is still fairly new to the organisation, but he's proven to be quite a good soldier.

"Bring them in alive. You'll have access to the private planes to get you on and off the island. I want this done as soon as possible." I push to my feet because I can't focus on anything but knowing we are going to end this fucking war soon. But also, I have a wedding to prepare for, and I need to sit with my future wife and plan what will happen on the day.

As the men file out, Val and Kai sit back and watch Brielle.

"Are you going to kill my father?" Brielle's voice is low, a whisper as she speaks. There is fear drenching her words. As it should be.

I haven't planned what I'm going to do with him yet though, but I will make an example of the man who tried to fuck me over. The thing is, it's not the first time he's been a traitor, so what's going to stop him from doing it again?

"I don't know. I don't have any answers for you yet," I answer Brielle honestly. I've always offered her transparency. Even when I scared her, I have never lied to her. Even though she's hidden shit from me, I never want to hide anything from anyone in my life. We may not yet be married, but I believe that a relationship is built on trust. And I want to be as open and honest as I can be.

She sighs softly and shakes her head. She must know how this is going to go because she's no stranger to this life, even though she led us to believe she was. "I know he started a war—"

"He did, and I don't think he's actually sat back and thought this plan through." I keep my tone even, before I look at her and continue, "And he's fucked up. I will be honest, if I were to kill him right now, I wouldn't have an ounce of guilt."

She looks at me then, and I realise, even though he's fucked her over, she still loves him. To be fair, I get it. My father wasn't the best man, he did nothing that could be considered *good,* but I still loved him. Looking up to a man who was bad to the outside world, I didn't think anything of it. But now, watching Brielle love her father even after all he's done, I understand it.

She's changing me. I don't like it. But I can't stop it. I've tried fighting it since the first day I met her. I wanted her to leave, to run far from Black Hollow and me. It didn't help that Valen had grown attached, and then slowly, Kai seemed to accept her while I was still at odds.

"I want to be there," Brielle announces suddenly as she looks at me. "When you bring him in. My father needs to look in my eyes and tell me why the fuck he's done this to me. He needs to explain himself, and then…"

She meets my gaze, and I can see the strength simmering in her stare. The girl who first walked into that office all those months ago is no longer in front of me. Instead, she's a woman. She's now ready to be a queen, and she's ready to stand beside me.

It's been a roller coaster, but I have a feeling that Brielle was a good choice. My father knew what he was doing, even though he had no clue she'd change the way she has. My chest tightens when I think of Dad. I don't allow memories to haunt me, but there are moments I realise that even though he's gone, deep down, he's still with me in so many ways.

"You can be there as long as you need to be," I tell her. "You'll get the answers." It's a promise. One that I never thought I would offer her, but right now, I want to see her smile.

Fuck this.

I have feelings.

I glance at Kai, then Valen, and they're both fucking smirking at me. They can read me. We're all trained to see tells from anyone we're questioning, but there are ways to see someone who is out of their comfort zone, and right now, I am.

"I don't see a problem with having Brielle

question her father. But we will need to be present. I'm not leaving you alone with him," Kai says as he looks at our girl.

She is ours.

There is no longer a doubt in my mind. She's proved herself once, and I have a feeling she'll do it again and again. Even though I still feel tense around her, I think it's more to do with me than with her.

"Your father will die," I tell her as I push my chair back and rise to my full height. Glancing over my shoulder, I offer Brielle a smile which is not filled with humour, but instead, drenched in a dark promise.

"I have no doubt," Brielle replies as she steps to the side, her eyes boring a hole through me. Something about the way she looks at me reminds me of just how vulnerable she makes me.

My father taught me that emotions make you see-through. When you allow your feelings to show, people can see down to the very soul you're wanting to hide. And I know Brielle has played her cards right. She can see who I really am.

"Meeting adjourned," I say as I push to my feet and walk around the table toward Brielle. Her head tilts back, and she glances at me with a gentle smile on her lips.

"Am I forgiven?"

I place my hands on the arms of the chair as I lean in and meet her pretty stare. "Would you like to be forgiven? Would you like us to take you to the bedroom and show you just what you mean to us?"

Those beautiful eyes hold me hostage. I never once denied myself a woman, even when I was younger and found my place at this school. I shouldn't have been as promiscuous as I was, but without my father watching over me, I was.

But when I finally admitted who I was, that I wanted both my best friends and we took that step. It changed everything for me. I didn't expect to want someone else. There was never a moment in my life I thought I would marry.

"There is no doubt in my mind that I'm yours. That I belong to the three of you and I need you all to believe me. I want the trust you show each other."

Her voice is firm, confident, and I can't help but smile. She's so beautiful when she's so fiery. There's a feverish need of desire that's coursing through me as I look at her. The idea of her taking all three of us at the same time passes through my mind.

"Perhaps you should come with us then," I suggest as I push away from the chair and straighten. I don't find it easy letting someone in. Deep down, it fucking scares me, which is why I didn't trust her when she first arrived.

I offer my hand, and smile. It's not a friendly gesture, it's a challenge. One I know Brielle will accept because she enjoys the push and pull.

Her slender hand slips into mine, and I pull her to her feet. I lift my gaze to Valen and Kai.

"Do you think she's ready for this?" I smile at my best friends because they know what this means. There hasn't been a moment in our lives where we've accepted a woman into our triad and taken her all at once. When we're all inside her. When we're joined together, it means we're claiming her completely.

"Are you sure you want this, princess?" Valen says as he tips Brielle's chin back with his index finger. The movement is slight, and her gaze locks on his.

"Give me the chance to prove to you, to all of you," Brielle whispers.

My chest tightens and my stomach twists when I consider that this is the next step. I wanted this from the moment I saw her, at least, that's what I now realise. Even in my hatred of the situation my father put me in, she had already captured my attention.

"Then you'll do so," I say as I snake my fingers with hers, and lead the way out of the office. Kai has her other hand, while Valen walks beside me. Excitement fizzles in the air with every step we take.

Instead of going to my bedroom, I lead her to her room. The place she'll feel most comfortable, but also, the space that she's come to know as hers.

When we finally reach the room, I stop in the middle of the room and we circle Brielle. She did good getting the information we wanted. Even though she had to figure out a way to hide the folders from everyone there, she passed the first test. Then, when I finally made sure every man in that house knew she belonged to me, I was less uneasy.

The clans can be volatile when they think they can step in and take what's mine. Fuck, I did the same when I was younger. But this is different, because we're all soon to be Bosses.

The only thing left now is to find her father.

I know it's not going to be easy, and when the time comes, Brielle is going to have to make a choice when it comes to the old man.

"You're sure you want this?" I ask once more. I'm not in the habit of forcing anyone to do something they don't. And this woman is going to be my wife.

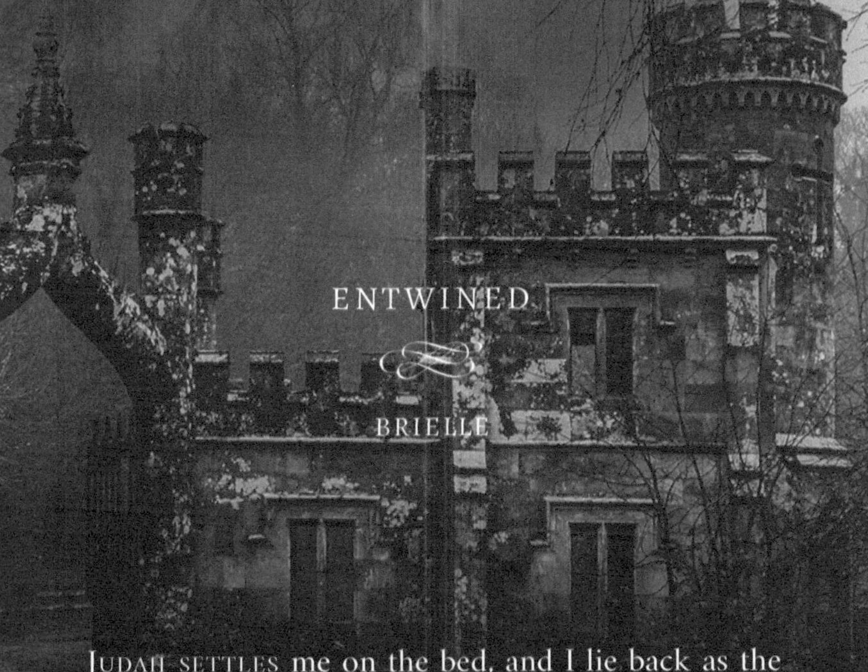

ENTWINED

BRIELLE

Judah settles me on the bed, and I lie back as the three of them join me. Kai leans forward, his hands on my hips as he teases my underwear down to my ankles. Judah watches me as he pulls Valen closer, and they kiss. Their tongues tangle together, and I can't deny I love watching them together.

Kai's fingers trail up my thighs as he pushes my legs open, and my hips rise from the mattress. My hands are already tugging at my top and soon it's discarded on the floor beside the bed.

My chest tightens, my heart slams against my chest as Kai's mouth captures my nipple and he sucks on it gently at first, then his teeth bite down. Goosebumps rise across my body, and his powerful hands push my thighs open.

"Please," I beg as I look into those eyes that always hold so many secrets. I want to know everything about them. My need to delve deeper with each man consumes me as Kai's mouth moves down my body until he's nestled between my legs.

Judah breaks the kiss with Valen, and they look down at me. Reaching for them, I allow my palms to run gently along their hardened erections.

"I want all of you," I whisper. It's the first time in my life I've wanted something so intense. Just the idea of it makes me squirm as Kai's tongue laps at my core.

He stops, lifting his head to look at me. Three sets of eyes regard me with interest. My request must have surprised them, because it's shocked me. I didn't expect to need them like this, all three of them at once.

"You want us to claim you, princess?" Kai whispers from between my spread thighs. "No running, no going back once this happens. You will have to be loyal to us only."

Even though I would do anything for them, I know I have to fully submit my heart and soul to each of them. I love them. It's not because my father forced me to marry Judah, and it's not because I hate my father for what he did. With this experience, seeing people's true colours, especially my father's, I realise I need to make my own choices in life. I can't listen or trust what everyone else tells me.

"Yes," I finally whisper as Kai inserts two fingers inside me. The feeling of being filled, stretched when he adds a third digit makes my back arch off the bed. Judah moves then, pushing his boxers from his hips down to his thighs.

Valen follows suit and soon enough, they're both naked. My hands instinctively reach for them, my fingers wrapping around thick, hard cocks. I'm not sure how I'm going to take them both, as well as Kai, but I need this.

Kai doesn't relent his ministrations as he takes me right to the edge, then stops, he continues this pattern of torture until my thighs are shaking. And as I lean toward Valen, then Judah, allowing each of them to use my mouth for their pleasure. Alternating their flavours on my tongue sends me into orbit when Kai pinches my clit and my core pulses around his fingers.

"Fuck," the curse word comes from someone, and I want to smile but stars dot my vision. "Such a pretty little spy." I recognise Judah's voice as I come down from my high, the need for more overwhelming me.

Someone shifts me slightly, and Judah lies back. Valen's hands hold me steady as I lean into his muscled frame. I look over my shoulder at him, and I smile. Then I look toward Kai, who's licking my juices off his fingers. The action causes me to blush. It's an erotic sight.

"You're delicious, princess," Kai informs me with a sly grin on his face.

"Are you ready?" Judah asks, capturing my attention. His left hand gripping his hard shaft, the tip glistening with his arousal, and I take a deep breath.

"I'm ready." I shift on the bed, straddling Judah, and I feel him at my pussy, the thickness of him stretching me. As I slowly sink down on his cock, I tremble with need coursing through my veins. Once I'm fully seated on Judah's erection, Kai moves to the top of the bed, where he kneels beside us, and then I feel the wetness. Valen's gentle touch massages the cheeks of my butt as he drips lube over the tight ring of muscle. With slow movements, I feel him insert a finger, or his thumb, and already the sensation overtakes me.

"Oh fuck," I murmur as I lean forward, laying myself over Judah's chest. My nipples against his chest, and he holds me so close, so affectionately, I'm stunned.

Valen adds another finger, and he works me open with ease.

"Just breathe, little spy," Judah tells me, his voice soft, caring, and for a moment, I want to tell them. I want to say the words that are on my tongue. But I wait because I can't focus on anything other than the fact that Valen now has the tip of his cock against me.

Every second that passes, I'm filled more and more. Valen doesn't thrust quickly, instead, he inches into me, stretching, opening, and filling me. His hands grip my hips, fingers digging into flesh, and my eyes roll back the moment he stops all movement.

"You're so fucking tight," Valen groans, his voice feral, like a wild animal and I have a feeling he's struggling to hold back.

Kai moves closer, and I reach for him. With the movement of my body, I can't help but whimper at the fullness. I've felt nothing like it. And then I take Kai into my mouth. All three of them, we're all joined. We're together.

Then the guys move. Each one slowly pulling out, then thrusting in. Judah's mouth captures my one nipple, then the other. He teases them with his teeth as he bites down gently, then laps at the hardened buds. Again and again.

Kai's hand tangles in my hair as he pulls me down on his cock. The gagging sounds that echo around the room are entwined with the groans of all three men.

I'm in heaven. I didn't think it was possible to feel so wanted, so possessed, but with them taking me, claiming me, I'm nothing more than a vessel.

I'm lost to the pleasure as they move, thrusting, fucking me, using me. But it's not only for their pleasure, I'm flying as my eyes flutter closed and I allow the sensations that are coursing through my veins to take a hold of me.

"You. Are. Ours." I'm not sure which of them say this, and I attempt to nod. But I can't move. Kai's hold in my hair is fierce, his fingers gripping strands and tugging until there are tears in my eyes. But there's no pain, I'm not afraid of them.

I want this.

I crave this.

"Ours." Another voice comes from somewhere. I no longer care as they move faster and faster.

"Forever."

"I'm so fucking close to coming."

I open my eyes to look down at Judah, and the silky flesh that slides over my tongue has him grinning.

"Such a pretty, little spy taking our cocks." His words make my core pulse. "Getting claimed and owned by the three of us." He continues with a salacious grin. "Our fucking Queen that's going to come for us. Aren't you?"

A hand snakes around my neck, Valen's fingers tightening on either side as he squeezes the air from my lungs with every thrust. I'm about to scream, but no sound comes out as my body convulses.

"Fuck." Kai groans as he pulls from my lips and I feel the warmth of his release hit my cheek, then my breasts as he finds bliss with his hand tightly wrapped around his cock.

Judah leans forward and laps at my tits, taking Kai's white hot release onto his tongue, and then he kisses me.

Valen's hand is still tight around my neck, while Judah shares the salty arousal with me, and then Valen grips my hip harder with his other hand, and slams into me, sending me cresting over the edge.

I pull away from Judah and cry out as my orgasm slams into me. My eyes shut so tight, I see white behind my lids. My body convulses, shaking and trembling, as I feel each of the men still inside me throb and thicken. Valen slips from me and the warmth of his release drips down where I'm still joined with Judah.

We don't move for a long while. At least, that's what it feels like because my body is nothing more than pliable flesh. My legs feel like jelly when I attempt to move.

"Are you okay, princess?" Valen whispers in my ear. I don't know if he's moved from behind me, because my eyes are still closed. All I want to do is pass out right now, I'm so tired.

"Yes," I croak. My voice is still raspy from trying to suck in air. I want to beg for sleep, but I feel hands shifting my body, and then I'm scooped up into powerful arms. "Where… Where are we going?"

My lashes flutter, and I see it's Kai carrying me. He's smiling down at me as he walks us to the bathroom. Judah is already there, as he turns on the shower.

"We need to clean up, then it's bedtime," Valen says when he joins us.

My mind is still catching up with everything that just happened. Once I'm settled onto the tiled seat in the large shower, all three men take over the space, and suddenly, it doesn't feel so big. It's Judah who crouches in front of me, and he cups my face in his hands.

"Are you okay?"

I nod, then smile looking at each man. "I'm more than okay." It's the truth. I've never felt like this. It feels as if I'm flying, and I never want to return to earth. "I want so much more of that."

All three of them chuckle at my admission and my cheeks burn from embarrassment. "Oh, trust me, princess," Kai says, "there will be much more of that for the rest of our lives."

That makes me smile. I can't believe I want this, I can't believe I'm even living this life right now. But I wouldn't want to be anywhere else.

Judah pulls me to my feet, but doesn't release my hands. Kai takes the shower gel and lathers it between his hands, before he gently massages my shoulders. Valen works on my front, with slow gentle movement.

I'm speechless as they wash me. Fingers exploring once more. But I can't help wincing when Kai's finger teases my arse.

"It's okay," he says when he hears the hiss that escapes my mouth. "I'm just teasing you slowly. Cleaning every inch of you." His tone is calm, nothing like the usual gruffness that he exudes.

Valen is in front of me, his fingers teasing my pussy while Judah tweaks my nipples. All of them have the softest touches, and soon I'm aching for more. I know I can't survive all three of them again, but they slowly build me up to an orgasm once more, but as I'm about to dive from the edge, I'm left wanting and needy.

"What are you doing?" I ask breathlessly as they watch me. All three men are now surrounding me. This time, it's Kai who takes the lead, and he turns me around before he settles on the small tiled bench. His cock hard, ready to enter me, and I realise what he needs.

"We don't—"

I cut him off by leaning in and pressing my lips to his. Even though he was in my mouth, finding pleasure, he didn't fuck me. I turn my back to him, and I reach between my thighs to grip his shaft before guiding him against my core.

Slowly, I sink down on him. His stubble against my shoulder when I lean back and feel the thickness of him deep inside me now.

It's when I look up do I realise it won't be long before I have that elusive orgasm they were just taunting me with. Watching Valen and Judah kiss, while they slowly stroke each other is one of the most erotic scenes.

"Do you like watching, princess?" Kai whispers in my ear as he reaches around and teases my clit with his thumb. The slow, methodical circles have me squirming on his lap as he taunts me.

I've always been open-minded about sex, about love. But seeing them together right in front of me is sensual. Two muscular bodies, two alpha males who would burn down the world for me, enjoying each other, takes me to that edge I'm aching to leap from.

"I think our princess wants to feel more." Kai's voice is strained, and I'm pretty sure he's going to come soon. "She likes to watch."

Judah and Valen look at me, smirks on their handsome faces as they step closer, and I'm able to touch them. They each grip their cocks, and I watch closely how they stroke themselves. Teasing the tip of their shafts, before teasing the arousal and I can't stop myself from leaning in and tasting each one.

And then I move. I slowly ride Kai's cock while Valen and Judah's hands move faster as they look down at me.

"Ours." Judah's voice is tinged with the darkness I've come to know from him. "No going back now, little spy." He doesn't take long before he shoots his release all over my tits. The same way Kai did moments earlier. A groan of pure pleasure rumbles in his chest, like a lion roaring and marking his territory.

When I look at Valen, he grins at me. The playful joker I've come to know is back. He follows Judah's lead, and marks me with his seed.

"Do you like that, princess?" Kai questions as his lips tease a trail down my neck. He reaches for my breasts, and he massages them, the cum making a mess of me, but I don't care. I'm so lost in the pleasure that's burning in my veins, the electricity that's coursing through my nervous system, I'm close to my own orgasm.

"Yes," I hiss as my head drops back onto Kai's shoulder, and he brings his cum-stained fingers to my lips, and I suck them clean. Licking and lapping at each digit like a starving kitten. The salty flavour bursts on my tongue. And when he pulls his fingers from my mouth, he uses both hands to grip my hips and slam into me.

His cock hard and thick, throbs inside me as I feel him groan. The vibration in his chest is right against my back, and I know he's about to fill me up as well.

It doesn't take long for another orgasm to hit me

and I'm shaking as I moan out the words that I held back earlier.

"I love you." I open my eyes, and smile. "All of you. I love you, Judah, I love you, Valen, and I love you, Kai."

And I know there's never going back.

Not because I'm forced to stay, but because I want to.

DEEPEST CONFESSION

VALEN

My chest tightens at her words. The three of us are silent for a moment, and I'm pretty sure Judah and Kai are in shock, just as I am.

I drop to my knees in front of her, and I cup her face in my hands. Even though the water is still spraying us with warm prickles, I realise I'm about to say something I haven't said to a woman before.

"I love you too."

Judah joins me in front of our girl and he takes her hand. Bringing it up to his mouth, he presses a kiss to her knuckles before he says, "I love you, even though I want to fight it."

And Kai's arms wrap around her, holding her close to him as he whispers in her ear, "As much as I didn't want to"—he pauses for a moment—"I love you too, princess."

I'm not sure what's going to happen once Judah and Brielle get married, but I know one thing for sure, she's ours.

When I think back to my own parents, I know I never told them I loved them. Not even my mother when she would look after me when I was sick. But then, I grew up and was thrown into this life. I didn't have the heartache Kai had been through, and I wasn't drilled into like Judah was, but my own past is still there, haunting me to this day.

And I know I'm going to have to tell Brielle at some point. I'd much rather not tell her anything. She doesn't need to know the shit I was put through. But if Kai can confess his past to her, I know I can.

When we finally get to bed, I'm exhausted. Cocooned between Brielle and Kai, with Judah on her other side. My eyes close, and I can't help but smile at the closeness of all of us. There were moments over the past few months that I was convinced this wouldn't work.

But now, I know it will.

I just need to sit Brielle down and tell her about my past.

WHEN I WAKE UP THE NEXT MORNING, I OPEN MY EYES to see Brielle still asleep. Judah and Kai are gone. They must be in the office, which gives me the privacy to talk to our girl.

I scoot up and sit with my back against the headboard. Knowing what I have to tell her makes me anxious, and my stomach somersaults when she finally opens her eyes and looks up at me. A small smile dances on her lips, and I'm tempted to kiss her. I don't though. I wait for her to fully wake up, her eyes staring at me as if she's just woken from a wonderful dream.

"Good morning," Brielle whispers as she leans in to kiss me on the cheek.

"Did you sleep well?" I run my thumb over her plump lower lip, and I steal a quick kiss before she can respond. For a moment, I linger there, wanting to taste her. How I'd love to spend the morning in bed, making love to her. But we have work to do, and before that, I have to confess. It's been hanging over me like a heavy weight for weeks now.

"It wasn't too bad. I was rather tired after last night." Her confession causes her cheeks to darken to a soft, rosy hue.

"Mmm, I wonder why," I tease her as I chuckle at the sweet shyness she exudes. She has these moments where she's fiery and confident, but there are instances where I look at her and I see the innocence still inside her.

I hope she never loses that. Because once you break free from that part of yourself, there's no going back.

"Are you okay?" Brielle questions, the concern in her voice is evident as she regards me.

"We need to talk," I finally say as I pull her closer. "I wanted to sit you down later, but since the other two are working, I figured now is the best time."

"Something is wrong," she murmurs as she reaches for my face. The gentleness of her hand against my cheek has me leaning into it. This girl can end wars with just a tender touch.

"Not wrong necessarily." I close my eyes and lean my head back against the headboard, before I look at her again. "I needed to tell you about my past. You should know what brought me here, to the island."

"Well, Kai told me about his past, and I accepted it. I mean, I know we all have our moments of weakness, we all have histories we may not want to talk about. I don't ever, won't ever, judge anyone on what they've done."

Her sweetness is too much for me. I want so badly to see her smile with unwavering happiness. Because as she looks up at me now, I can tell she's nervous. She's worried about whatever it is I'm about to tell her.

"When I was younger, I grew up much the same way Judah did. My folks watched me like a hawk. I was meant to walk in my father's shoes the moment I turned twenty-five, but something happened not long after I turned thirteen."

Closing my eyes, I recall that night so distinctly, it's as if I'm there right at this very moment. I hated what happened, and I buried it deep. The only people who know what went on are Judah and Kai. Of course, my parents will never speak of it again, and now that I'm no longer in their home, I wonder if they even remember just what they did.

"You can tell me anything," Brielle whispers softly as she holds my hand.

I swear on my life, this woman is a saint. She's an angel sent from above to look after us. I'm sure of it.

"It was the first time I took a chance and kissed someone else. It had been a long time coming, and I had been fighting with my own feelings for so long, I thought I was going mad."

My chest tightens as I recall the moment I felt

lips on mine. I didn't know about love, or lust, or any of those emotions. All I knew was I wanted to kiss him so badly, I couldn't stop myself from leaning into the kiss that night.

"My birthday party was in full swing, and even though Judah and Kai were there, they had wandered off with girls from our private school. At the time, we didn't want to admit our feelings for each other."

I look down at Brielle who's now watching me with rapt attention. Her focus on mine as she bites down on her lip, it's as if she knows something is about to come, and it's not going to be good.

"What happened?" Her voice is nothing more than a murmur of fear and trepidation as she speaks.

"There was this boy at our school, he wasn't one of the princes, and I thought, I didn't care at the time who his family were. We had been friends for a better part of that year, and as we sat watching the fireworks, we smiled at each other, and then it happened."

"You kissed?" There's a glimmer of hope in her eyes, her voice takes on a newfound happiness, but I know it won't last long. The thought twists at my gut.

"We did," I tell her with a nod. "It was then I

realised I wanted to explore. It may sound strange at thirteen, but I knew who I was. I didn't expect to feel anything, I thought perhaps I was broken, but it was the first time I felt remotely *normal*."

"But something happened. I mean, there must be more to it than that. Did you end up dating each other?" Once again, it's that optimism that makes me smile at the princess. She's so perfectly innocent it makes my heart thud against my chest.

"We didn't," I tell her in the silence of the bedroom. "It wasn't easy coming from the family I did. I know Judah's father was tough on him, and Kai's adopted father is just as strict, but mine..."

I allow the quiet to fill the space between us. Just for a moment, I don't want to continue. The memories assault me painfully, and no matter how much I fight them, I know they'll always be a reminder of what I witnessed.

"Did your parents find out?" Brielle speaks so softly, I barely hear her, but with the thoughts racing through my mind, her gentle tone cuts through all the bullshit and heartache.

I nod.

"Oh, Valen," Brielle moves closer against me and rests her head on my chest. I didn't think I would ever want to be comforted like this, but having her here makes this bearable. It sounds so strange to me to even think it.

"They saw me that night." I swallow back the agony, the memory burning right through to my soul. It was the first time I realised how much I hated my father. My mother wasn't any better. She stood by, but then again, even if she did try to stop him, it would have been detrimental to her. He was a bully, a man who didn't care what he did, as long as he got his way.

"Valen," Brielle's voice once more cuts through the darkness that's taking over, and I glance at her. "What happened?" This time, she shifts to her knees, instead of leaning her head on my chest, she watches me with confusion.

I'm not sure how to even voice the next part of the story without allowing rage to fill me. I fisted one of my hands, the need to hit something running rife through my veins. My gut churned with the desire to make him pay. Over and over again.

My father is still alive, even though he's not the man he used to be. They say karma takes her time, but when she doest strike, be fucking scared.

"Valen, what happened?" Brielle now even more concerned leans in close, and the darkness that had descended on me slowly dissipates. Her calm, sweetness overwhelms me and for the first time in years, I allow my tears to fall.

"My father decided it was a good idea to make a spectacle of the boy I kissed. Of course, I couldn't live my life how I wanted. And for me to be anything other than a straight, alpha male in my father's eyes, was wrong."

"Oh no." A tinge of sadness, of regret, and of pain drenches those two small words that Brielle utters. It's obvious what had happened next. Well, to most it would be. But the details are far worse than she could ever imagine.

"It wasn't that night though. But I knew what was coming because he told me. My father was livid. I was locked in my bedroom for two days, until they brought Diamo to the house. We had a similar setup like the Venier's where my father had a basement where he took those he wanted to interrogate."

"And the boy you kissed, Diamo—"

"I didn't realise he was there until Judah sent me a text message and said my father's men were at the school. They picked him up and left." I allow myself to look at Brielle who is as stricken as I was when I read Judah's message that day. "My father didn't call for me until late that night. I had screamed, banged on the door, but they didn't let me out."

"So you… Your father allowed you to see him?"

I nod as I swallow back the lump in my throat. Deep down, I realise just how tortured I was by it. I think the shock, the fear, and the heartache that had overwhelmed me had me bury the moment I saw him deep. Because when I close my eyes, it springs up suddenly. It wasn't there all those years ago, but now, I can see it clear as day.

"My father had him chained to a table. He was already beaten badly." I choke out the words, forcing them to spill from my lips because if I don't, I'll never allow them to escape. And as I confess the rest to Brielle, I go back there.

"You see what happens to boys who break the rules," *Dad says to me as he sneers down at the innocent boy. I can't believe I've done this, put someone in danger because of my own confused feelings. Emotions are fucking dangerous.*

"Dad, please, you don't need to do this."

"Don't I?" he challenges me and I know he wants me to break. My father believes to strengthen someone, you need to bore down into their soul. He enjoys watching me shatter. All my life, he would punish, then buy me something to show me he loves me.

"No. Honestly, it was a mistake and it won't happen again," I tell him, praying silently that he'll believe me. I could never lie to my father though. He grew up with venom in his veins, trained by the most dangerous mercenaries who worked for the mafia. When he took over the family, he didn't bat an eyelid when he needed to torture or kill someone.

He basks in the violence. And now, as he turns to the boy who's begging for mercy, I know he'll show none.

"Please, I didn't—"

The crack of my father's fist against Diamo's face has me recoiling. The bone is broken. I heard it break. The bile that I'd been swallowing back rises quickly, and I'm bent over, puking my lunch up as I drop to my knees.

"Do you see what you've done to my son? Making him weak with stupid emotions he shouldn't be having for the likes of you," Dad hisses in a low, feral tone. He's no longer human, he's an animal. Livid, I swipe my hand against my mouth to clean myself and push to my feet.

I run at my father but he's fast. He sees me coming before I make contact, and his knuckles slam into my face, right under my left eye. There's blood dripping from the cut from my father's ring, and I'm holding onto my cheek as I look up at the man I thought was my hero.

"You will watch," Dad says, and two of his soldiers hold me steady. As much as I try to struggle out of their *grasp, they're bigger and stronger than I am. There's no escape.*

I shake my head as I look at Brielle. My mind in the present, shoving the image of the next few moments away. I don't want to think about it, but I have no choice.

"He made me watch as he tortured Diamo. For hours. He cut him, then poured vinegar into the wounds. He rubbed salt on burns he created with a lighter. Everything he did, I saw. He made sure I didn't turn away."

"Oh my God," Brielle gasps when I finally break down and I allow myself to cry. My shoulders shake as she holds me, wrapping her slender arms around me. "I can't believe someone can be so evil."

I know she's still getting used to this world, but I know that what my father did wasn't the worst. I've definitely heard of terrible stories from other children. But, it was also the worst thing I'd ever witnessed in my life.

"Where is your father now?" Brielle asks, pulling away to look up at me. There's a glint of fear in her eyes, and I don't fucking blame her.

"Karma came for him about three years ago. He

suffered a stroke first, then once he believed he was healed, he was adamant that I couldn't take over from him. So, instead of allowing me to do his job, he was determined to show the world he was still a bastard to be feared. He went out on a job to meet with some contacts who shot him. He's in a coma and has been since," I tell her.

Her mouth pops open in shock. "So he's alive?"

I nod. "My mother doesn't want to pull the plug."

"Wow."

"Which is why we're so careful to keep our secret. Once we're in our new roles, it will be easier to come out. To show the world who we are. And to make sure that nothing like what happened to Diamo ever happens again."

I'M STILL IN SHOCK. The story that Valen told me has been bothering me since yesterday. The moment I step into class, I'm bombarded with the scent of cologne. In the front of the class is Professor Toscano who started a few months ago.

He's still getting all the attention from the handful of female students who attend the school. There are rules in place to ensure that he's not allowed to date any of them, but I still wonder if he's been tempted by someone.

"Hey, girl," Emilia says as she slides into the chair beside me. I haven't seen her in a while, and I wonder why.

"What had you away from school for so long?" I ask as I arch a brow.

This time, she giggles in response. "I may have met someone. But I can't talk about it," she says quickly. "Maybe we can have a girls' night after your big day. I mean, once you're back from the honeymoon."

"Oh, I don't think we're going away for that," I tell her. The idea of being whisked off the island, and taken somewhere exotic has crossed my mind, but Judah doesn't strike me as someone who would do that.

"Oh please," Emilia says with a wave of her hand. "There is a chance you may never come back. I mean, with the money and connections Jude has, I'm pretty sure he'll be the one to sweep you off your feet."

She sure has a different view of the man I'm about to marry.

"Maybe."

We're interrupted by class starting, and I turn to face the front. I'm going to have to pass if I'm going to graduate. Even though I'll be working alongside Judah, I want him to see me as an equal, not just a girl who's around the house all day doing nothing.

My dream has always been to be independent. I didn't want my father to be taking care of me all my life, but I also didn't expect to be getting married while still at university. We can't plan our lives, not in the world of family obligations and organisations. But I'm thankful Judah hasn't set any rules out for me. He hasn't forbidden me to study, or to graduate, and I can't deny that it made me look at him differently. I was convinced he would try to lock me in the fucking basement if he had to.

Granted, he has done it a couple of times. But, I'm sure we've moved past that stage of our relationship. The distrust must have dissipated by now. He has to realise I'm not running, and I'm not going to do anything to put them in any danger.

"Hey," Emilia's voice draws me back to class and I realise I'd drifted off with thoughts of weddings and the boys. "You haven't made any notes."

I glance down at my notebook and sigh. "Shit. Can I copy from yours?"

She giggles at me once more, and nods. "Of course. I can't deny, if I were you I would have taken some time off school to prepare for the wedding."

"It didn't even cross my mind," I tell her earnestly, the idea of not coming to class doesn't sit well with me. But the countdown is over, and the wedding coming up tomorrow is an event in my life I can't change.

"Shouldn't you be home right now making sure

your dress fits?" It makes her laugh when I roll my eyes in response.

"Oh please, I haven't changed much in the past few weeks. I don't know," I finally say. "I'm just not one of those girls who had laser-focused plans for her wedding. To be honest, I didn't think I would ever get married."

Emilia's eyes widen in surprise at my comment. "Really?"

I nod.

"I was the girl with the scrapbook of photos and dried flowers, and bits of fabric pinned to every page. I planned everything." There's both excitement and embarrassment in her voice, and I wonder why I never thought about things the same way she did.

"I suppose I grew up with my father, and it was definitely not something I had anyone to talk about with." I shrug it off. "But I knew a lot of girls at school who did. So, I think we're all unique in our own ways."

For a moment, she ponders this and then nods with a smile. "You're right. I mean, if we weren't all so different, the world would be a much more boring place to live."

I want to agree with her, but then I remember Valen's story. My chest tightens and my lungs struggle to pull in air when I imagine what he felt that night. At times, being different is good, but then there are those moments when it can be detrimental to all those involved.

"Yeah," I say absent-mindedly.

"Don't forget to send me photos when you're back," Emilia says as we leave class, but before we step outside, she glances back and I notice the look between her and the professor. I wonder if he's the person she mentioned earlier. He's so much older than us.

But I'm not one to judge. As long as they're both happy and consenting, there isn't anything wrong with dating someone who isn't exactly *perfect.* I've learned that over the time I've been on the island.

We can't choose who we love, the heart has a mind of its own and fighting it only hurts in the end. And the most difficult thing I've learned is that judgement kills.

"I'll bring them all over on a drive so you can watch them on a loop," I tease her as we make our way to the parking lot. The deep rumble of engines captures my attention, and I notice Judah and Kai both here in their racing cars.

"Looks like someone is in for an adventure," Emilia laughs as she bumps my shoulder with hers.

She's sweet, and I make a mental note to spend more time with her when I'm back from the wedding. I'm not used to making friends. When I lived in London, I was more focused on passing with high marks than partying with any of the girls.

But since I'll be living here indefinitely, I should lay down some roots. And I'll definitely make sure to befriend more of the girls who attend the school.

"I'll see you soon," I tell Emilia as we say our goodbyes. When I slip into the passenger seat of Judah's car, he doesn't greet me. Instead, he pulls out of the parking lot with a loud squeal causing me to slam back into the expensive leather seat. "What the hell is going on?"

He glances over at me, arching a dark brow. "I'm dropping you at home so you can prep for tomorrow. The team is waiting."

"The team?" I squeak as I pin him with a glare. "What team?"

"I have girls at the house waiting to make sure you have your full body massage and spa treatments ahead of tomorrow. They'll also do your manicure and pedicure tonight. Saves time in the morning."

"You're acting like I can't do this—"

"Tonight is about you relaxing. I don't need you to be walking down the aisle feeling tired and sluggish. Also, you'll go to bed early tonight." He doesn't look like he's joking. There's a dark commanding threat in his voice that makes me sit back and sigh. "Don't do that."

"Do what?" I don't look at him as he rests a hand on my thigh. "I just didn't think I'd be away from all of you tonight."

"I'm out with the guys. But I'm not staying out late," he informs me. "We're getting some drinks and heading up to the cliff."

"And what if you fall and die?" I throw back as frustration takes a hold of me. This time, I do look at him, pinning him with a glare.

Judah chuckles. "I won't die. Besides, I'm about to promise to annoy you for the rest of your life," he says then, a smile prominent on his face. When he's serious, he's beautiful, breathtaking even. But when Judah Venier smiles, my heart isn't ready for it. Perhaps it's because he does it so rarely.

"Fine," I huff before I sit back and cross my arms in front of me. "But if you're late tomorrow..." I leave the warning between us, and I can hear him chuckling.

"All three of us will be there," Judah promises, causing me to look at him and I can see the emotion in his eyes. I didn't expect him to ever look at me the way he is right now. It makes my heart skip a beat.

"I'll be good and obey you this once," I tell him. When Judah finally drops me off at home, the three of them change cars, and the driver takes them off into the evening.

I didn't expect him to plan so many things for me. As I reach my bedroom, there's a masseuse bed waiting on me already. It's a special gift, something thoughtful, and I wonder if it was Judah who thought of it, or if it was Valen.

"Principessa," one of the soldiers knocks on the open door before he walks into the room when I nod. "This arrived for you." He hands me a large envelope, and gives me a friendly smile before he disappears down the hallway.

I'm looked after. Guarded like a prize in this home. I feel safe though, and that means a lot to me. I settle on the bed as the masseuse gets the oils ready and open the envelope.

Inside there are two smaller items. One carded envelope that's addressed to me, and one to Judah. The curiosity has me already tearing open mine. I'll leave Judah's for the morning, because I have a feeling when he returns tonight, there won't be much focus from my future husband.

I fold open the pages which are thick vellum. It looks like it's been written with one of those ink quill pens. On the top centre of the first page, is a symbol, the Venier family crest.

My chest tightens and my heart thuds at what this could be. I allow myself to get lost in the words on the page.

Dearest Brielle,

I will be honest with you, a Saviatti in my home doesn't sit well with me. But, when the time came to choose someone for my son, I knew who it had to be. Not only because I know the type of person you are, but because you grew up outside this life.

You may hate me, and that's no surprise. I would hate me too if I were told one day I'd be marrying the mortal enemy of my family. But there was no choice when your father asked for my help. I needed to ensure he would abide by the rules I set out for him. Perhaps by now, those rules are forgotten, but I have to trust that he will ensure you're safe no matter what.

Our bloodlines run deep, and pride in our

family name is important, but by now, you would have learned who your father is. The man you grew up with, who raised you to the young woman you are, has not shown you his true nature. I tried to keep you and Emilio safe, as safe as can be in this world.

You don't have to take my word for it, but you'll learn as time goes by. When I sat with the options for Judah's bride, your photo was there, in the myriad of pretty faces. I knew you would challenge him because you were a fiery little thing. And I will be honest, I had watched you for years. I needed to know who the woman was that my son would take to his bed.

It may now sound strange to you, but that's how this world works. One day, perhaps, Judah may have to choose a partner for your children. It's how things work. I do hope though you'll forgive me for the intrusion on your life.

I brought you to Black Hollow to meet Emilio, to build a relationship with the brother you never knew. I won't go into detail on how all this will play out, but I've seen it for myself, and I know you'll be good for my son.

Things may not always make sense, but I wish

you a beautiful wedding day. May there be no blood spilled, and may your future be bright. Don't forget where you've come from, but also, don't forget to look forward and move away from the sins of the past. We all have to do it, and those who don't, will pay.

There are so many more things to learn. Time will tell and it will teach you both. Trust in Jude, he'll look after you. And all I can do is pray that you'll care for him too.

I hope that my choice has been a good one.

Blood, honour, and loyalty,
Till Death,
Omertà...

I'M STILL STARING AT THE WORDS WHEN THE MASSEUSE calls me over to the bed. Quickly, I put the letters away, and as I lie down, I wonder what Judah's letter says.

His father chose me for a reason. All my life I thought I was safe from this life, from this world, but I was being watched. He knew more about my father than I do, and even though he did, he still chose me for his son.

I don't know if that makes me happy, or sad. I

think I am quite sad that I'll never get to meet him face-to-face. I'm also saddened that he'll never get to see just how much I truly do love his son.

But for him to have written that before he even met me, must mean he could read me as a young girl.

The knuckles kneading my muscles don't calm the tension that's coiling inside me. The idea that Judah has a letter too has me on edge. Even though mine wasn't bad at all, I wonder what he would say to Jude the night before the wedding.

My eyes flutter as my muscles ease with the pressure the woman working my shoulders adds. At least I'll be able to sleep tonight. Perhaps I'll go to Judah's room and sleep there. Wait for him.

Who knows what the future holds, all I can do is wait until we find my father and speak to him. He needs to explain, and I need the answers to all my questions before I know he will meet his maker.

He's lived on the run for too long, and he's tried to mess with the family who helped him time and again. I no longer feel guilt in knowing that soon, my father will die.

And I have to go on.

No matter what.

Omertà.

I DON'T COME HOME and expect to find Brielle in my bed. I thought she'd be asleep in her room, needing space for the last night of her single life. Even the thought of that makes my stomach twist with both excitement and anxiety.

She looks peaceful as she lies under the covers. Her long hair fanned out over the pillow as she breathes deeply. The room is only lit by the one bedside lamp. I want to wake her, but she's calm and relaxed, and I know if I did wake her, she'd only ask a million and one questions about where I've been.

It was a rather quiet evening. I told Kai and Valen I didn't want something crazy. Perhaps I am growing up, maturing, like my father wanted me to. Maybe it's Brielle's influence.

Knowing that tomorrow I'm going to say *I do* to her has me wondering what thoughts she had running through her mind tonight. Even though I planned the massage and the spa treatments for her, it couldn't have been easy to be on her own.

Deep down, guilt twinges in my gut. I should have stayed with her. At the very least, I could have invited one of the girls from the school, the one she's always talking to, Emilia. But I didn't think about it until we had arrived at the cliff edge.

By then, I'm pretty sure she was already lost in her massage and relaxing on the bed. One thing about the girl I realised I had fallen in love with, is that she's happy in her own space. She doesn't need people around her to feel at peace.

I like that about her. It shows her strength, her calmness to work solo. It's how I have been for years. Granted, I did have Jordan to stick around and help when I needed it. But for the most part, while I was at school, and as I was learning from our father, I did it on my own.

I unbutton my shirt while keeping my gaze on the angel asleep in my bed. I don't know why my father chose her, or how he even came across her name, but I can't deny, I'm glad he did. Something about her has changed me, and at first, it scared the shit out of me, but now, I'm ready for the challenges that life will bring us. Because I know there will be fucking roller coasters that will try to derail us.

The thing about it is, with my new family, the four of us will get through anything life throws at us. I didn't want to admit to the guys earlier, but the love I feel for them, as well as Brielle hasn't weakened me in the slightest. Even though I was convinced it would.

No.

It's strengthened me more than I thought possible.

Once I'm stripped down to my underwear, I slip under the covers, and Brielle stirs ever so slightly, but I don't wake her, thankfully. Instead, she wraps herself around me and I can't help but fucking smile.

I'm not a pushover, but I'm fucking weak for her. And I will kill anyone who tries to hurt her, or take her away from me. But it's not only me, Kai and Valen would do the same for her. She is ours and I couldn't be prouder.

She has given herself to us.

I feel the shadow at my bedroom door and I see Valen and Kai watching us. The smiles on their faces tell me everything I need to know. We've found our missing part. She fits perfectly like a missing piece to the whole that we tried to be on our own.

As soon as the guys leave, I close my eyes and hold her close. Tonight we're sleeping alone, but tomorrow will be the start of something brand new. An adventure neither of us saw coming, but we've accepted it, and we now welcome it.

I OPEN MY EYES TO FIND BRIELLE WATCHING ME WITH a soft smile on her face. Her eyes are shimmering in the low light of the sunrise that's slowly streaming through the curtains.

"You're so peaceful," she whispers before pressing her lips to mine. Fuck, the taste of her is like a drug. I want nothing more than to spend hours, days, weeks, just enjoying her body, her flavour. But we have a shit load of things to do before the ceremony.

"You shouldn't be stalking me," I throw back when she pulls away and I meet those pretty eyes.

"To be fair, it is part of my job now." She shrugs as she gets off the bed and makes her way over to the window where she pulls on the curtains to open them further. "There's something I need to give you.

I wanted to wait up for you last night, but I was so tired, I fell asleep."

This intrigues me as I scoot up in bed. "Oh?"

She turns to regard me, the smile turning serious and my chest tightens. On one hand, I almost expect her to tell me she's leaving us. And on the other, I am sure she's going to tell me something that I'm not going to like.

"Last night there was a delivery. Well, it wasn't too late. Just after you dropped me off." She moves across the room and I watch her pull out a small envelope that was hidden on the side of the bed where she had slept.

"Who brought this in?" I ask as she hands me the item in question.

"One of the soldiers, I think his name is Romero. There were two sealed letters. One for me, and one for you." She looks at me as I lower my gaze and my heart stutters. The script which bears my name is so recognisable, I would know it anywhere.

"It's from my father?" This time, when I look up at her, I'm shocked when she nods. "You've read yours?"

"I did. I thought I should wait for you, but I was far too curious. It's a letter, somewhat explaining things, but also, leaving a lot of unanswered questions. Perhaps yours has more of an explanation than mine."

Brielle rounds the bed and heads to my side where she cups my face in her hand. She presses her lips to mine in a soft, affectionate kiss, and then she straightens.

"I'll leave you to read it. I need to go shower and get my hair and make-up done. And then, I'll see you at the altar."

"I love you," I blurt randomly, and I want to pull the words back into my mouth. I don't know why I said it, but I felt the need overtake me. I've never said those words to anyone other than Kai and Valen. I didn't even say it to my father.

As I think this, I wonder if he knew I did actually love him. For all his faults, he was a good father. He was nothing like Valen's fucking arsehole of a dad.

Brielle smiles at me, then whispers along my lips, "I love you too, husband." And then, she turns and leaves me with the letter in my hands.

I'm scared to open it. I don't want to know what my father's last words to me would be. The idea of him writing something that would break my heart doesn't sit well with me.

I haven't told Brielle about the fear I had of letting him down. It's something that was painfully obvious when I was younger. But as I got older, I hid it well. And now, I realise it's not even noticeable anymore.

Perhaps she's already noticed. Maybe she has seen my weaknesses and she loves me anyway. I don't know because I never asked and if I had to be honest, I don't want to know. If it turns out she doesn't know about how fearful I was as a young boy, it would only cause me to push her away because I wouldn't want her to see my truth.

Then again, she's accepted me with both Kai and Valen. My thoughts are a jumble as I rip open the envelope and I pull out the thick vellum paper my father used to enjoy using for all his contracts. He used to handwrite everything. He always said it had more merit when it was handwritten.

Dear Jude,

You must be sitting at your desk, or perhaps you're in the garden reading this. If it's your wedding day already, I want to wish you all the happiness in the world. If it's the night before, remember, to live your life without abandon. Either way, I'm sorry I can't be there with you right now.

You may hate me, and that's okay. I've come to terms with it. I wasn't a perfect father. I did things that were questionable at the best of times, but I hope you realise why I chose Brielle for you.

You spent your life living in my shadow. I could tell you worked hard to want to please me, to make sure you didn't disappoint me. Yes, you were fairly obvious when it came to it, but I want to say to you now, you never disappointed me.

I spent my life proud of both my sons. And when I took my final breath, I knew that the Venier name would live on in everyone's mind as a strong, domineering force within the world we come from.

And that's why I chose Brielle. When her father asked for my help, I drew up the contract. It was something I didn't want to do, but I thought, it can't be too much hassle. And then I watched her grow up. I always had eyes on my payment. Or rather, your payment.

She was a strong-willed, independent woman. I knew the moment she turned sixteen I had made a good choice. She will challenge you, she will change you, make you feel. I want that for *you. It's what your mother did for me. But she's also a soft and kind-hearted girl, which will match perfectly with your hard exterior. It's something you got from me, and it's something I hope you never lose.*

But I will say one thing—don't ever push her away with that rough personality of yours. I know for a fact that the match is perfect, if, and only if, you can let her in.

Be a good man, and she'll be a Queen for you, Jude.

Rule with an iron first, and love with a soft heart.

Blood, honour, and loyalty,
Till Death,
Omertà...

It's only when I set the letter down do I realise I'm crying. I don't feel these things, ever. But right now, I'm a fucking emotional mess.

Pushing off the bed, I make my way to the attached bathroom. I need to get ready, and when I do, I'm going to finally obey my father's wishes without so much as a debate in my mind.

I NEVER GET NERVOUS.

I don't think about myself as a worrisome person, but waiting for Brielle to walk down that aisle has me on edge. With Kai and Valen, and my brother standing beside me, I should be at ease. The guests watch me, I can feel their eyes boring into me, but I don't turn around because if I do, I'll end up walking out. I can't do that to her.

It's been months since she first walked into our lives. I didn't want her, but she was given to me, a gift from my father. At first, I was confused as to why he would have given me this woman, because she's no longer a girl. The beauty who will be Mrs Venier, is a strong, intelligent woman, and I'm proud to call her ours.

When the organist starts the song, I know it's time. I don't want to turn around, but I can't stop myself. My chest is tight as I glance around, and see her at the entrance to the church. Getting married on Black Hollow Isle was Brielle's idea. I figured she'd want to go to the mainland, but when she told me how much this place has come to mean to her, I couldn't disagree.

The whole island is mine, but I share it with Kai,

Valen, and now her. We're the ones in charge, and that's not going to change anytime soon.

I've never wanted for anything in my life. Whatever I asked for, my father provided, and in his dying wish, he has given me a forever. Granted, he didn't know about my relationship with Kai and Valen.

I don't know what I'm doing. Walking into a married life with someone, with three someones, wasn't part of my plan. I don't think it's part of anyone's life plans, but here I am, watching the girl I love walk down the aisle.

She looks like a fucking angel.

The floor-length white dress has full skirts, and the bodice is a corset made of lace and embroidered with diamonds. With every step, Brielle shimmers like a beacon in the darkest of nights. Her long hair has been pinned up, but there are long, wavy strands which frame her delicate face. Her features are almost pixie-like as she smiles.

Her gaze flicks around the church, and she takes in every person. I'm saddened her father couldn't be here to walk her down the aisle. I'm sure it's every girl's dream, but she doesn't seem at all upset, or perturbed that she's doing it alone.

Beside me, Kai and Valen stand with their backs

straight. All three of us waiting on her. The moment she comes to a stop in front of me, she looks over my shoulder to the two men who she's promising her life to, and then to me, the husband who will join her in this sacred ceremony.

Today is our day, and in a week, I'll step up into my father's role as Boss of the Venier family with her at my side.

"Are we ready?" The priest asks as we turn to face him. Brielle holds my hand, and I tangle my fingers through hers. I can't deny it, I'm scared. Not in a bad way, but I'm nervous that something is going to go wrong. My gut churns as I silently pray that nobody will disrupt proceedings. Because that's the last thing we need today of all days.

It's Brielle who answers first, "We're all ready." It may sound like she's talking about us, and the guests, but only the four of us knows she's talking about the unique relationship we're committing ourselves to.

"Then we shall begin. Welcome to all those gathered here today. It's a momentous occasion when two people fall in love, and they agree to walk the path of holy matrimony."

I'M ABOUT to get married.

As I stand across from Judah, and I watch him look at me, my heart thrums in my chest. There's a lump in my throat that's been there since I left him this morning. I haven't seen him since I left him with the letter. But as he offers me a smile, I realise it must have been good for him to read it.

"If there is anyone here who thinks that this union must not take place, speak now, or forever hold your peace." As the priest utters the words, the lump that has been choking me since this morning feels as if it's about to take me out completely.

But as silence greets us, I sigh a breath of relief. "You both have chosen to write your own words of promise."

Judah nods and he pulls out a small scrap of paper, and I almost giggle when I notice just how nervous he really is. I thought it would just be me shaking like a leaf, but it seems he's just as anxious as I am.

"There have been many moments in my life that I had disagreed with my father's choices. He asked me to do something, and I would refuse, but I also spent my life not wanting to displease him. Even though I challenged him, I knew that one day, I would see life through his eyes."

Judah stops, then looks at the guests, and offers Jordan a grin. The brothers are so similar, but they're also so very different in many respects.

"But today, I stand here before you, Brielle Saviatti, and I'm obeying my father without debate. It's the first time in my life that I agree with him wholeheartedly."

This makes me laugh, and the guests join in as they chuckle. There is a lightness to the congregation, and it seems happiness has filled the small island church.

"I take your hand today," Judah continues, "And I promise to hold it through the darkest of times, and the best of times. There will be ups and downs, sickness and health, and I can't deny there will be times you'll want me to leave you alone. But, in all those moments we go through, we will still do it together."

I promised myself I wouldn't cry, but his words tug at my heart, and I can feel the tears burning my lashes as I fight them. I don't want them to fall, not yet because I have my vows to go through.

"When I place the ring on your finger, and when we're pronounced husband and wife, you'll have me at your side forever. Not only as your husband, but your best friend, your confidante, your bodyguard, and the father to your future children. I promise you all of me. And I give you my heart. I love you, Brielle."

I can't fight the tears, because they fall free, and Judah reaches up to swipe at my cheeks. The smile on his face sets all my worries aside, and I can't wait to kiss him. I want to do it right now, but I know I have to abide by the proper procedure.

"How am I meant to top that?" I whisper which makes everyone laugh.

"You don't have to top it, you just have to mean what you say." Judah's reassurance has me grinning. Never in my life did I think I'd be here willingly marrying him.

I take my small note card tied to the bouquet, and

I open it. I don't look up at him, because if I do, I'll burst into tears.

"Judah," I whisper his name, before I start, "when I was brought to Black Hollow, I didn't consider it my home. I tried to look at the future, and it never included this small island. It didn't include you." The lump in my throat is back, and I have to fight to swallow past it to continue. "But now that I'm standing here, in this beautiful dress, and looking at you, I realise how blinded I was by the anger at the situation we were thrown into."

Judah takes my hand, and he holds it firmly. It's as if he can tell I'm too nervous to continue, but he's my rock.

"I've always believed things happened for a reason. Life changes swiftly, and when you least expect it, your eyes are opened to possibilities you didn't know you would want, or need. And that's what happened with you. I didn't know I wanted you, or even that I needed you. But as time passed, and we grew together, it became clear that you're someone I cannot live without."

I swallow again, praying I'm not going to puke all over my dress. Lifting my gaze, I quickly flick it over Valen and Kai, and they both offer me a nod. They know I'm talking to them too.

"I'm giving you my heart, as I take yours. I'm giving you my life, as I join with yours. And I promise to love you, no matter what life throws at us, expected, or unexpected. I'm on this roller-coaster ride with you, and I'm not getting off."

There's a silence that hangs in the air for a moment before the priest asks, "Do we have the rings?"

"Yes." Valen steps forward with the ring I have for Jude, along with Kai who has my ring.

"Judah, repeat after me, Brielle Saviatti…" And as we go through the motions of the required vows, and the rings are slipped on I realise that there are some dark days ahead before we can finally find our happiness.

My father will soon be found, and even on this beautiful day as we are pronounced husband and wife, the *presence* of him is still around.

We walk back down the aisle toward the exit with Valen and Kai following close behind. I would gladly run off now and leave the island for a few days, but we have a reception and guests to greet before any of that can happen.

It won't be the first time people are invited into the Venier mansion, but it is the first time it's for a wedding. The guys used to have parties there all the time, but that was when they were single. It is rather strange to think I married one man, but I get three instead.

I am a lucky girl.

When we get back to the house, I head up to the bedroom to change into another dress, while Judah follows me to help with the corset.

"I'd much rather we stay here and I can properly undress you and make you my wife."

I laugh out loud. "I'm already your wife," I remind him as I turn in his arms and press my lips to his. "But we can't be rude. We have guests, and they've travelled all this way to be here on our special day."

Judah rolls his eyes, but he nods. "Fine, but tonight, you're ours and you won't be leaving the bed until you're nothing but a pliable mess." There's no threat there, only a promise. Another vow on a day when I'm all vowed out.

"I would expect nothing less from you, Kai, and Valen."

Quickly, I change into a white trouser suit and make my way down to the party where the guys are entertaining the guests already. They're laughing and drinking, and when Judah and I walk in, we're met with a chorus of *whoops* and whistles.

I grab a glass of champagne, while Judah lifts his

to the guests. There's a smile on his face, but I can tell he's not in the mood to be friendly to people. He wants to be alone which only makes me feel all warm and fuzzy inside.

"On behalf of my lovely wife and I, we would like to thank you all for being here today. It means so much that you travelled from far and wide to be here today. I hope you enjoy the party, and please, have fun."

We move through the room, smiling and laughing with those who wish us well. I don't know many of the faces in attendance, but as they introduce themselves, I realise there are far more dangerous allies than we have enemies. At least, I hope so.

By the time we finally get a moment to ourselves, I gulp down the wine I'd been holding for an hour, and I lean against the floor to ceiling, glass patio doors. The garden is faintly lit with the yellow glow of the torches that were lit for those who wanted to go outside for fresh air.

The autumn breeze is chilly, and I watch as some huddle together with their cigarettes. I never saw the point in smoking, it's not something that ever interested me. I'm thankful for that now because I'm indoors, warm.

"You're beautiful," the soft whisper comes from my left, and I turn to find Valen smiling at me.

"Thank you." I place a hand on his shoulder, and give it a soft squeeze. I hate that we have to hide our relationship, but I also understand why. "I wanted nothing more than to have a quiet evening with all of us celebrating," I admit.

Valen nods, a smile on his lips as he regards me. "I know. It's not easy when you have duties to fulfil. This is probably how the royal families feel when they're supposed to obey and smile through ceremonies."

I can't help but laugh. "I don't think I'm all that royal. To be fair, I don't think I could do this all the time. There is only so much you can do to plaster a grin on your face and act as if you're interested in what people are saying."

"That's true," Valen agrees. "But, as the Queen of the Venier clan, there is much more to the role than just smiling. And in a few days, there'll be another ceremony, this time in Italy where we'll be around many more family members than I would like."

There's a sadness in his tone, and I wonder if his mother will be there. I don't ask because I don't want to sadden him further. Instead, I smile and whisper, "Well, as soon as everyone leaves..." I allow the promise to filter into silence, and those gorgeous eyes that have always intrigued me dance with amusement.

"Now you're just being a tease." Valen laughs out loud, the sound filled with happiness, and my heart swells as I look at him.

"I think it's time to call it a night," Judah sidles up to my side, and slips his arm around my waist.

Kai saunters over to us, and lifts his tumbler. "A few of the guests are leaving, it won't be long until there's silence in the house again."

"Now that is music to my ears." Judah's gruff tone is back. Long gone from the sweet, affectionate words he spoke earlier. We're very much the same, we prefer our quiet time. The idea of having to spend all night and day with strangers sets me on edge.

Especially when I know we have so much work ahead of us. The thoughts I pushed back earlier slam to the forefront of my mind. My father is out there, and I know we'll find him soon enough.

The only question is, when we do, what's going to happen. I have no doubt I'm going to learn a lot more about the man who raised me than I care to want to know.

Judah's phone vibrates and rings in his pocket.

He releases me with a curse of, "Fuck," before he pulls the device out and swipes to answer. "What?"

He listens, but steps away and out into the garden where it's quiet. My heart rate spikes when he looks directly at me, the darkness in his gaze returns. I know what it means—they've found Papa.

I'm pretty sure our honeymoon is going to be put on hold for the time being. Judah speaks to whoever it is, and I turn to the guys who are also watching him.

"Brielle," a woman's voice comes from behind Kai, and I see it's one of the wives of a Capo who works for us. *Us.* How strange to think that way. "Thank you ever so much for the wonderful day. Congratulations again."

"Mrs Romano," I offer with a smile as she leans in to kiss my left cheek, then the right. "So lovely to have met you."

"You mustn't be a stranger now. When you're on the mainland, you let me know and we'll go shopping and have some lunch together." She grips my shoulders and offers them an affectionate squeeze.

"I will, thank you so much." I've never really had a mother figure. I wanted to know what it's like to be like the other girls who had doting moms, but it wasn't in the cards for me. Perhaps, within this sordid world, I can find some form of a maternal connection.

"Of course! We can always gripe about the men too."

"Oh, please, you love us," her husband teases from behind as he offers me a handshake, then kisses both cheeks as is customary.

"Thank you for being here. Judah is just on a call."

"I'll see him soon for the ceremony," Mr Romano says with a wave of his hand. "Tell him I said to not be late."

"I will."

Once they say their goodbyes to Val and Kai, they're off, and slowly, each couple, and the soldiers in attendance leave.

By the time Judah is off the phone, I'm so tense, my stomach is in knots. He steps up beside me, his arm once more around my waist, but there isn't a gentle affection to his touch, instead, it's a tense grip.

"They found your father trying to flee Naples." His voice is low, angry, and I can tell that the happy day has now been soured.

It's a good thing though. He's been found and he will be brought to justice. I just wish it wasn't on my wedding day.

"Are we going to Naples?" I ask as I look up at Judah who has a livid expression on his face.

"As much as I want to say no, we will stay home and celebrate, I think we should go. Once this is all over, we can take a month off and just travel the world."

"I agree with Jude," Kai says with an affirmative nod.

Valen sighs, and replies, "It's going to be for the best. We can get the answers we need out of him. I think the fact that we can put this to rest now, is best. Especially before the ceremony where you take over the organisation from your father."

I know they're right, but I still want to pout. I still want to stamp my foot and refuse to do anything other than spend the night with the three of them.

But, I also need the answers to the questions that have been racing through my mind non-stop.

"Let's go."

Judah looks at me as we settle in the car and says, "Mario helped." I didn't expect him to say my brother had anything to do with finding Brielle's father.

"He was the one who called?"

Judah nods. "He said that he had a team out searching because he had an inkling her father would go to the Camorra after I married Brielle."

This intrigues me because it doesn't make any sense. If I were him, I would have stayed clear of the men who I almost sent to prison. "Why? He fucked them over. Wouldn't they just kill him?"

"I thought so too." Judah shrugs and then looks at Brielle. "Do you know of your father's contacts in Naples?"

She shakes her head, her hands tangled in her lap. "I don't. I thought he would have gone back to London, or even the States. Since he was an informant, it would make more sense for him to go to those who helped us escape."

I don't miss the wince on her face as she says it. She knows her father isn't the upstanding man she believed. It can't be easy to know your father is both a liar and a killer.

Although, we still don't know what happened with her transplant. "Have you taken your medication?" I ask her suddenly as the thought pops into my head. We've been so focused on the wedding, and trying to find her father, we haven't checked on her.

"Yeah," Brielle whispers. "I never forget to take it. No matter what's going on around me. If I don't..." She doesn't need to finish her sentence because we all know what could happen.

Our girl.

I can't believe she's ours.

"Good." I sit back and turn my attention back to Jude. "I think we need to find out where exactly he was headed in Naples. There are a few clans in the city, but there are also the smaller organisations based around the world. They're worse than us."

The Camorra have always been more tyrannical, more dangerous than the Sicilian Mafia. There have been instances where the clans would work together as allies. However, the structure of the Camorra is far removed from those of its counterparts.

"Do you think they'll kill him if they know he's there?" Brielle's concern isn't unwarranted, but she has to realise her father walked into the lion's den. If he chose to go to Naples, there has to be another reason.

"We won't know anything until we talk to him, or find out from them directly." Judah's voice is firm, the confidence he exudes when there's a job at hand makes me proud to call him both one of my best friends, and the man I love.

By the time we're in the air, on the way to Italy, Brielle is pacing in the bedroom. I can hear her soft footfalls. I try to get a hold of Mario, but there's no reply. He's probably asleep or busy, but he has to respond at some point. Hopefully before we arrive in Italy.

"Do you think he's going to even admit to anything?" I ask Judah as I look over at him swallowing back the alcohol he poured. "A man like that always makes me wonder if he has any morals."

"He doesn't have morals. The thing is, I don't

want Brielle to be heartbroken when she learns the truth." He's really worried about this. I think Brielle will be strong, focused on the truth, but then again, parents have so much power over us, I can't truly tell her reaction. It may be worse than I think.

Pushing to my feet, I head into the bedroom to find her sitting on the bed. When she looks up, I can see she's been crying.

"Talk to me." I settle on the bed beside her and take her hand in mine. "You know you can tell me anything. There are no secrets amongst us. We're together now and it won't change."

She sighs softly, and then whispers, "My father wasn't a good man. He has done things that I'm sure I'll regret learning about, but it hurts my heart to know he couldn't sit me down and tell me the truth."

"Some people want you to see the best in them. They know they've done something wrong, so instead of confessing their mistakes, they hide them, or they force you out of their lives."

"Do you think he sent me to live with Judah because he was trying to get me out of his life, or out of the way?" In this moment, I can hear just how pained her voice is. She's broken up about this, and I can't imagine sending her away because of something I'd done. The idea alone makes me sick. Her father is a stupid man.

"Maybe," I say with a shrug. "You can't tell until you hear it from him. Until the moment he gives you answers, don't sit here alone and dwell on it. I know it's easier said than done."

We sit in silence for a long while, and I wonder if she's going to ever heal from this. Parents are people we look up to. We put them on pedestals, and when they don't live up to those expectations, we find it difficult to cope with.

My biological parents were pretty much the same leaving me with nothing. I was convinced that I wasn't worthy of love, but in the end, love did find me in the form of the Erranis.

"You know," I say to her, "we can go and relax in the front, or we could invite the guys in here and we can rest for the last bit of the flight."

Brielle smiles, and nestles her head into my chest. Her sweet scented perfume invades my senses and takes over my need to have her right here.

"You all make me feel so special," she whispers. "I don't know how I would survive without any of you in my life. To be honest, I didn't think I would ever be able to fall in love with any of you."

"How could you not love me, I'm delightful," I

tease her, causing her to giggle and I smile at the sound.

"I think I'd spent so long hating this world that forced my father out, I didn't expect to be back in it. And I certainly didn't think I would ever *want* to be a part of it."

"Lie back," I tell her as I rise and allow her to relax back into the bed.

"What are you doing?" Brielle whispers when I lean in and kiss her lips, then trail my mouth down her neck, over her collarbone. My hands gently tease her breasts, and I pinch her nipples enough to get a squeak out of her. When I reach her hips, I tug at her leggings, and along with her underwear, I drag those down her legs, and to her ankles. Once both items of clothing are on the floor, I spread her thighs.

"I'm having some fun," I tell her. "Do you want to be watched?" I whisper against her soft skin which makes her whimper.

"I-I-I don't know…"

"Jude, Val," I call to the guys as I press kisses to the sensitive flesh of her inner thighs. I move higher, and higher, and when I see the guys walk in, surprised by the sight before them, I allow my tongue to dart out and lap at the sweet essence of her pussy. She's already soaked, ready for more. I want nothing more than to have her coming all over my tongue and fingers, but more than that, I want to make her scream with my cock deep inside her.

"You like to be watched?" Jude whispers in a low, gravelly tone as he moves closer. He shifts onto the bed, while Valen takes the other side, both kneeling on either side of her head.

"I think she needs something to fill that pretty little mouth," Valen says before I thrust two fingers into her tight cunt.

Her slick walls pulse around both digits, and I circle her clit with my thumb, working her into a frenzy as she shakes and trembles.

She takes Jude's cock in her mouth, while she strokes Valen slow and steady. They're both wet and leaking, as she teases and taunts them with her perfect plump lips. I don't make her come with my fingers, the moment I feel her flutter, I pull both digits from her, and I rise to full height. Her gaze is on me, watching as she now takes Valen's cock down her throat. The sound of her gagging only makes my dick throb harder than ever before.

"You're our little slut, aren't you, Brielle?" I murmur in a raspy tone.

I'm so lost in the frenzy that's taken a hold of me, desire coursing through my veins, I don't care that

I'm being a filthy bastard calling her that. But she doesn't seem to mind, because as I tease her entrance with the tip of my cock, she practically fucks me back by lifting her hips.

"Do you want it, princess?" I tease, running the leaking tip up and down her core.

Her mouth pops off Valen to whimper. "Please," she begs, and I don't wait, I don't move slowly, I grip her hips and thrust all the way in. The one, fluid motion has her crying out as I bottom out inside her.

"Fuck." The word escapes from my lips, through clenched teeth as I try not to come immediately.

I have to still for a moment to catch my breath, before I can pull out slowly, and then thrust back in. When I start moving, I watch the erotic scene before me. Brielle taking both cocks that are weeping arousal, and she rubs their wet tips on her lips, before she licks the salty flavour.

"A pretty princess, our naughty little slut," Judah says, which only makes her pussy tighten around my cock. "You like it. Don't you? Being so filthy for us. Taking all three our cocks," he continues to taunt her and with each word he utters, the closer she gets.

I circle her clit once more, and I feel the flutters start. "Our naughty little slut is going to come all over my cock," I announce as I fuck her harder, deeper, faster. I push her legs back, and rest her ankles on my shoulders as I slide deep into her body.

With every thrust, I knock the wind from her. Both Val and Jude are close, their hands moving along with hers as they stroke themselves over her face and tits. Her nipples are hard peaks, and both men tease the little buds until I feel her come.

Her cry of pleasure echoes around us, bouncing off the walls as I thrust one last time, deep, and I throb inside her. She's painted with seed as Jude and Valen groan in unison, and I can't help smiling down as I look at her. She looks beautiful lying there, spent, her mind no longer on the drama that lay ahead, but on the bliss that's currently coursing through her veins.

I can't deny, sex does seem to help with a lot of life's problems. It's my belief anyway.

I slowly slip from her. We're going to be landing soon and we all have to freshen up. I wish we could spend more time in here, but we have a job to do. Unfortunately, life throws ice over our desire.

With the guys straightening themselves, I help Brielle up and into the small bathroom to refresh herself. Once she's done, she steps out into the bedroom and offers me a smile.

"I know what you did there," she tells me.

I feign a shocked expression. "Me? What do you mean?" I ask, playing dumb. But, she's far too intelligent for me to get away with it. I know she is.

"Thank you," is all she says.

"I'll do anything for you, princess," I tell her earnestly. "I would burn down the world for you. And I would certainly kill for you. There isn't any one that could take me away from you, unless I'm killed. But you have to know, all three of us are yours as much as you are ours."

She blushes as she listens to my confession. "I know that. I didn't before, but I do know that now. I think for me, I just wasn't used to the attention. Not from one, or three men. It's all new ground."

"It's new to us too. We've never had a long-term woman who we could share ourselves with." It's the truth. There may have been previous partners who walked into our lives and spent the night, but none were special enough for us to ask them to stay.

Granted, Judah was given Brielle by his dead father, but she has burrowed her way into our lives, into our hearts. We have given her the trust we couldn't give to anyone else.

"Do you think that once you're all stepped up into your roles you'll be able to come out and tell the world about us?" It's a question I've been pondering for years. It would be much easier to live a normal, open life, but with all the shit that the elders believe, it's not going to be easy to let anyone in on our lifestyle.

"I really don't know," I tell her. "There are so many threats that come with being in the mafia, and to add the interconnected relationship we have, it could be detrimental. When people know you love someone, there could be harsher threats than the one we currently face."

Brielle ponders this for a moment. "I suppose you're right."

We don't talk any more about it, as the plane descends into Naples, we all get ready to disembark. We're about to walk into what could be a life-changing situation for Brielle.

I don't know what's going to come of it, but I do hope that she receives the answers she gets. As we pile into the waiting car, I say to Judah, "I think Valen and I will go find the hotel and make sure the suites are ready. You should go with Brielle. It's only going to cause more issues if we all four go in there."

He looks at me then, "Are you sure? I think perhaps we will need you closer."

"You'll handle it, we trust you," I tell him with a firm nod of approval. The only reason I want to be alone with Val is to plan a little party for all of us once the ceremonies are over, and I want it to be a surprise for them.

We have so much going on at the moment, I think it would be nice to have some time to relax and not think about all the bad shit that's gone down.

Judah nods. "Sure. We will need about an hour. Wait out here for us and we'll find you when we're done." With that, we wait for them to exit the vehicle. Once they disappear into the enormous mansion, we pull away.

"What was that about?" Val asks, and I turn to him with a smile.

"We have to make a plan."

And I know that we're going to come up with something incredible. Because Valen loves a good party.

I don't know what to expect when I walk into the room, but it's not to see my father chained up. I don't blame them, he's done some shit in his life, and right now, I don't have any sympathy for him.

When he looks up at me, his eyes widen in shock. "What are you doing here?" His voice is pained, and the guilt dances in his gaze as he regards me. "You shouldn't be here. I knew that boy would bring you down and force you into a life you should never be in."

"You're the one who agreed to the terms and conditions, Papa," I bite out as I step in front of him and see my father for the person he truly is. The anger that had overtaken me when I first found out about the contract is back, but this time, included in those emotions is the pain I feel when I think about all the lies.

"I wanted you safe."

"No," I spit out. "You wanted *you* safe. Let's start right at the beginning. Care to tell me about my surgery?" There is a lot to unpack with my father. And I'll gladly stay here for as long as it takes.

When he looks away from me, I realise whatever we thought he had done, was true. My father hurt another girl, in order for me to live.

"I'm not leaving until you answer all my questions. And I don't want your sob stories. I need the truth." I don't shy away. In the past, I may have cowered if my father looked at me the way he is right now. But I'm no longer the little girl wanting to please her father. I can't be the daughter he raised, because I'm now a woman, and I have my own family to look after.

"Brielle, there are things about this life—"

"There are things about you that you lied about. I was near death, what happened to suddenly bring a miracle into my life and allow me to keep living." I step closer to my father, and I lean in to make sure he can't look away from me. "What did you do to that girl?" The question is enunciated slow, steady, and meticulously so that he can't deny anything. My father knows that I know.

"I wanted you safe."

"Tell me the fucking truth," I bite out through clenched teeth, and the surprise on Papa's face is evident. I've never spoken a word out of turn toward him, but I'm done with that because I need to know how I'm alive.

"Emilio's mother was a woman I was seeing for a few years." The truth that spills from my father's mouth has my stomach churning with disgust. "Your mum and I weren't even talking anymore. Sure, we lived in the same house, but that was it. I... I was lonely and I met—"

"What happened to the little girl?" I cut through his explanation because I don't want to know the details of how he cheated on my mother. Anger burns through my veins as I pin him with a glare so fierce, it's surprising he doesn't shrink back.

"I was desperate. You were my first born, my little girl."

"I wasn't your first born though," I remind him. "Emilio was."

My father nods. "You were my first and only

daughter and I couldn't lose you. At the time, I was working for the Camorra, and I told the Boss how worried I was about you. I was so deep in their clan I didn't see a way out. And when he offered to help, I accepted it without a second thought."

"So you had a child killed, so I could live?" I challenge him then. I feel sick to my stomach listening to this, but I know I have to. There is no other choice because I have to get through the darkness to look to a future with Judah, Kai, and Valen.

"Yes," he admits with a whisper of agreement. "I made a choice. And I'd make it again, over and over again. There won't ever be a time I wouldn't decide to ensure you live, Brielle. I won't apologise, and I won't feel guilty for loving you."

In some ways, I understand it, and in other ways, the heartbreak of what he caused to happen makes me angry. I would do anything for the men I love, but could I kill an innocent to save them. I'm not sure.

"So you ignored your morals to save me? What if I was meant to die? You messed with a natural order of things."

"Don't give me that new age shit, Brielle," Papa spits as he looks up at me, pinning me with a fierce stare. I know where I get my fire from, it's from him.

"It's not new age shit to have morals, to feel guilty because a little girl who was innocent, who wasn't even ill, is now dead because of you." I step back, the rage taking over me has me trembling, and I have to fist my hands at my sides.

Turning away from him, I focus on the wall on the far side of the room. I feel broken when I think about what my father did, even if he did it to save me. And deep down, I know I can't forgive him.

"Brielle, I had to do things to ensure you were safe. And when I went to the Veniers, I needed help to keep you alive for as long as humanly possible. Knowing that I may be dead soon, I had to make sure you were safe."

Spinning on my heel, I stalk toward my father, and look him directly in the eye. "You were so concerned with keeping me safe, but what about Emilio? You couldn't sit me down and tell me I had a half-brother. At the very least you could have been upfront with me."

"I know," he appeases. "I have made far too many mistakes in my life, but the one thing I didn't make any errors on, is the fact that I know you're alive, you're safe, and you'll have a happy life."

"Without you," I add as he finishes his admission. "I want you to tell Judah all the things you told me. I need you to explain how you used me to get to him. Because even though I tried, he needs to hear it from you."

Dad watches me for a long moment, and then he offers a nod. His gaze drops to my hand, and he smiles. "You're married now."

"Yeah," I whisper. "I got married today. Aren't you glad you soured the day for me?" I'm acting like an insolent child, but my anger has taken a hold of me and it's not letting go.

"I'm sorry for everything, Brielle."

"You know that the Camorra aren't going to accept apologies. They'll want to see your head on a chopping block." I cross my arms, needing some form of stability. And that's when I feel Judah's hands slipping around my hips. He doesn't pull me close, but I know it's a show of support, of reassurance that he's with me.

"It's time for you to come clean. Your daughter, and your son, have been through enough with the lies. I think perhaps you should remember that as their parent, being honest will only serve you in the long run." Judah's tone is void of all emotion. He's angry, I can tell. There's a chill that races down my spine when Judah releases me and steps toward my father. There is nothing to stop him from killing the man who raised me. Not even I can keep my husband from acting out what has been simmering beneath the surface for so long.

"I give my life for hers. Once I'm gone, she'll be safe with you." My father looks at Judah. "I knew she would be because your father made a promise to me."

"And what if I don't uphold that vow?" Judah challenges Papa, and I want to gasp, but I stay quiet. The shock of what Judah has just asked has me on edge. I know he loves me, so he wouldn't hurt me, but what's to stop him from getting someone like The Agency involved. They could so easily find me, kill me, and Judah could play the broken-hearted husband.

"You wouldn't," my father spits out as he scowls at the man who just recited the most beautiful wedding vows to me. It's as if both men before me are as volatile as each other. And I can escape neither of them.

Judah chuckles darkly. There's a hint of malice in the sound, one I recognise from the day he took me to the cliff's edge. When he promised me that he could easily end me.

He spins on his heel, and makes his way to me and within seconds, his hand is wrapped around my neck. His fingers slowly dig into the sides of the column which cuts off my breath.

My hands grip his one, but I can't pull them away. His eyes glower as if he's possessed and in this moment, I don't see my husband, I see the arsehole who first brought me to Black Hollow.

"It's so easy, Saviatti," Judah says, but he doesn't look at my father, his stare is locked on mine. Panic sets in as my vision is dotted with black spots.

"Please," I croak, before I turn my gaze to my father's. "Papa."

"Judah, stop," my father's voice is pained as he tugs at his bindings, but I know they're far too strong to break. He won't save me. "Fine. I'll do as you say."

But my husband doesn't relent. He leans in and presses his lips to my ear. "Trust me." It's two words, and in my mind, even though everything feels as if it's slowing down, my panic eases and I drop my hands to my sides.

"Please, Judah, fucking hell, I'll do anything you

say. I'll help you." The sound of my father's voice sounds so far away.

Judah gently eases me back to the present moment. When I open my eyes, he's looking down at me with pride shining in his eyes. "I'll never hurt you." He steps back and instinctively, my hand goes to my throat. I'm not sure if I'm angry or turned on at him, but either way, I'm going to slap him when we leave this fucking place.

Judah turns to my father, and then he says, "You will write a full statement of all your crimes against us. The Mafia, the Camorra, and everyone else you hurt. It doesn't matter if it's some random stranger you didn't know, or your daughter. I want it signed, in blood."

My father's mouth pops open, shock painted on his expression. I'm sure he wants to argue, perhaps debate with Judah, but I know there won't be changing my husband's mind. Papa's gaze flicks to mine, it's only for a second before he nods.

"I'll be waiting at a hotel in the city. Once you're ready, we'll return and we can finish this off." Judah turns to me, "Wait outside for me. I'll be right now. There's something I need to say to your father."

I want to argue, but I don't. Knowing Judah, he

won't budge until I've obeyed. Once the door to the room is shut, I can't hear anything. It only makes me more anxious. Moments pass, and I can't help but pace the corridor. Finally, after twenty minutes, Judah exits the room and he offers his hand. I want to talk to my father, but also, I don't want to hear the lies he'll tell me.

"What happened?"

"Nothing. We need to leave." He doesn't look at me. I wonder if he killed my father, but I don't ask. I'm not sure I want to know.

I take Judah's hand and we walk out, leaving my father possibly still chained, awaiting his fate. When we reach the car, my anger at Judah has dissipated and I'm left with the empty feeling of knowing my father will be dead in a few hours.

"How did it go?" Kai asks the moment we slip into the back seat of the SUV.

"Not as great as we expected, but I've left him with a task. If he can complete it, I may show him an ounce of mercy," Judah admits, causing my head to snap up, my gaze landing on his.

"You said he's going to die," I whisper while looking at my husband.

He nods slowly before glancing out the window as if lost in thought. When he turns his attention back to me, he answers, "He knows what I'm capable of now, there's no need to take things to extremes. Also, he may come in handy."

"Can we trust him though?" Valen questions. "If he fucked over the organisations all these years, he can do it again. And not to mention, you will have the Camorra coming after you if you show any form of mercy to an informant."

I don't want to, but I have to agree with Valen. Even though my father has apologised and agreed to do what Judah's asked of him, there is no way to trust him.

"I'll have his confession, which will go straight to law enforcement. The Camorra won't know until he's behind bars. Killing him would be too easy," Judah says then, before he glances at me. "The life-long torture that I've bestowed upon him for now will suffice. Don't worry, it's been handled. Keeping him alive, making sure he's witness to everything that happens around him is going to ensure he obeys, that he's loyal."

"And you want to keep him alive to taunt him for however long he survives?" Val asks, his tone incredulous, but also, there's a hint of a chuckle that I can tell he's stifling at the moment.

"I have a feeling that you sent me out of the room for a reason. I want to know what it is," My voice is tinged with confusion, but also, the demand is there. However, my husband only smiles and his gaze flickers with something I can't quite pinpoint and all I can do is sit back and sigh.

"I need you to trust me, little spy." Judah looks at me. I can tell he was serious when he held me close and begged me to trust him. The thing is, I do trust him.

"I'd like to see my father again. To say goodbye."

"We can go together to get the signed confession from him," Jude responds. "And then, we'll head back to Black Hollow before planning our honeymoon. I want to go away somewhere, far from the island. We need to put the past behind us."

"I thought I would feel more hurt," I say as the car pulls away and we head to the hotel. "I think I'm just angry."

"Once the anger fades away, you will feel the heartbreak. It's not easy to accept someone you think you know is lying to you." Valen's words hold more meaning than he's letting on. "At times, you want to see the best in others, but there comes a point in our lives we have to accept that nothing is always what it seems."

Nodding, I lean forward and take his hand to give it a squeeze. "But looking back won't change the past," I say then. "Once all this is over, we will only look forward." It's a small promise. I can't heal his past heartbreak, but I can love him now until my last breath, and show him that he's a good person. He's nothing like the man who raised him, just like I'm nothing like my own father.

STEAL MY BREATH

VALEN

WHEN WE GET HOME, the place is surprisingly quiet. Usually there are staff wandering around, or Jordan is here with one of his many female friends.

"I'm thinking about the room downstairs." Brielle's voice catches me off guard when I turn to find her walking into the living room where Judah and Kai are relaxing on the sofas.

I flop into the armchair, and we all three look at her, waiting for her to elaborate. She's still stricken from seeing her father which is understandable. From what I heard there are many more instances where he played God when he needed something done. The first of course was with Emilio's little sister. Over the years he took life into his hands and he toyed with it as if it were nothing but a distraction.

"What room, princess?" Kai asks when she doesn't continue.

The apples of her cheeks darken to a deep red, and I realise then what she means. It's the dungeon, the room we bound her in and toyed with her.

"The one with the cross," she says as she sits on the arm of the sofa where Kai is currently sprawled out on.

"Oh?" He pushes up, and then glances at me, then Judah, before looking back at Brielle. "Are you in need of punishment?" he questions, tipping his head to the side.

We haven't really used that room for its intended purpose with anyone else. Brielle is the first female who has been in there. Usually, it used to only be the three of us who would play in there.

"Maybe," she whispers as she tugs at the hemline of her top. She doesn't look at us, and I wonder how she can be such a seductress, but also so fucking shy at the same time. It's like she's been made to tease us, and we're barely moths, flying far too close to her flame.

"You want to go back down there?" Jude asks her as he leans his elbows on his thighs. "Because I'll gladly take you back to that room and make sure you forget all the nasty shit that you've been through today. And I'm sure the guys will agree with me."

"I am most definitely in agreement with that." I can't deny, the idea of having her bound at our mercy is a delicious thought. I've never been one for any harsh treatment, but watching her come, over and over again, then begging for us to show her mercy before we each fuck her, that sounds like an evening of well earned entertainment.

"I'd like that very much." Brielle's blush darkens further as she regards us. "I want to forget. I want to clear my mind, and find some form of normalcy, in the mess that's currently taken over my thoughts."

Judah is on his feet, and he makes his way to Brielle. He takes her hand, and Kai and myself follow them down to the basement where I'm already anxious to experience this with her.

IN the basement we move into the room where the large, wooden St Andrew's cross still stands against the wall. It wasn't that long ago that we were in here, binding her to the implement. Only, this time is far different, because Brielle has asked to come down here.

"Strip," Kai orders her, taking a step in Brielle's direction. "While we're in here, you are to obey each of us. There are no questions, and no debating. However, you will choose a safe word. If something is too much, if you want anything to stop at any time, you will call this word out. Am I understood?"

Brielle shivers at Kai's commanding tone, but she nods. "I understand."

"What is your safe word?" Judah asks as he pulls out some toys from the drawers. Two plugs which shimmer under the low lights, a wand, which I know will be fun. And he's also brought out the crop. I recall Brielle's cries of bliss when we used it on her before.

"My safe word is *spy*," she says shyly.

Once Brielle is naked, she looks at Kai, awaiting her next instruction. It's Jude who takes the next step and he picks up the lube, and the smaller butt plug which he removes from the packaging. It's brand new, been in the cabinet for so long, I forgot about it.

"Time for the princess to wear her jewel." There's a salacious smile on Judah's lips as he regards her. "You'll have to bend over right here, and I want you to hold onto the table."

"Will that hurt?"

"Not more than when you took all three of us," I inform her as I move to get the wand. I want to have the first few moments of seeing her squirm.

Judah works slowly, teasing Brielle with his fingers, then he inserts the small silver toy. Once it's in, there's a soft whimper from our girl. It's a sexy, erotic sound she makes and my dick is already throbbing to be inside her.

"Stand," Kai orders as Judah steps back, and he moves with Brielle to the cross. Soon enough, she's bound by her ankles and wrists. This time, there is no fight from her, she's smiling as she watches me lift the wand and step in front of her. Thankfully when I turn it on, it's charged. I close the distance between us, before I set the slow vibrating tip to her nipples, and as they peak, Judah and Kai work them as I move the wand over her stomach, down to her mound.

Each inch I lower the tow, Brielle moans, her hips now rolling, undulating to put more pressure against the vibrations. But I move it away, and she snaps her glazed stare at me.

"Naughty little slut," I murmur along her lips. "You'll wait until I'm ready to make you come," I tell her as I press the toy against her clit this time which has her crying out.

The sound of her nearing the edge is like a sweet song in my ears. Her lashes flutter and I look over to Kai who offers me a nod. We're going to send her over the edge multiple times. Until she taps out. She'll call that safe word because I'm sure she can't take too many orgasms.

I keep the wand at her pussy until Brielle's release shatters her from head to toe. She's shaking, her whimpers and mewls bounce against the walls. But I don't move the vibrating toy. Instead, I leave it on her, and smile when she looks at me.

"How much can you take, princess?" I challenge her, knowing that we're going to push her to the very edge.

"As much as you have to give," Brielle breathes the words as her chest rises and falls.

I chuckle at her fire, and reach down to slip two fingers into her tight little cunt. "So wet," I remark as I thrust into her. The vibration of the wand is still humming against her as I tease the spot inside her that has her thighs shaking.

"Please," Brielle whimpers as her head drops back and she shuts her eyes so tight. There are tears at the edge of her eyes as she tugs at her restraints.

"Look at me," I command her, my voice low, a deep rumble, and when our pretty princess looks up, I turn the strength of the toy up a notch and it sends her over the edge so quickly, her scream is high-pitched, and it's drenched in shock.

Her eyes widen as she glares at me, but she doesn't call out her safe word. She can at any time and this will stop, but I know she'll fight it for as long as she can.

Her juices drip down over my hand, and I pull my fingers from her, Kai grips my wrist, and he looks directly at her as he licks and laps at the wetness. He takes two digits into his mouth, and they lock eyes as he sucks her release from my fingers.

"Delicious," he murmurs and I hand Judah the wand, but he's already got the crop in hand when I step back and he takes over.

"It's time for a little pained pleasure, little spy," he tells her before running the leather implement over her lips. "Kiss it."

I'm sure she's about to fight him on the order, but after a moment, she presses her lips against the tip of the crop.

"Such a good, needy girl," Judah praises her, before he swats her one nipple, then the other with the leather, causing her to mewl out loud.

Kai and me watch as the black toy trails its way down her body, leaving small rosy pink patches over her porcelain skin. With every swat, Jude presses the bullet he has in his other hand against her clit. But he doesn't keep it there, he only teases her.

And then he reaches her mound with the crop, and the swat is loud, causing Brielle to scream.

"You can stop me anytime you need." It's a reminder from Jude, but she doesn't do it. There is no safe word uttered.

He spanks her again with the leather crop, and with every pained slap, he teases her clit with his fingers. Over and over again until she's dripping arousal down her inner thighs. The sight of her at our mercy is more than dick-hardening. I could probably come just watching this scene play out before me.

Then, Judah holds the bullet against her and doesn't move it. Brielle squirms, and I'm sure she's trying to get away from him, but he doesn't relent. There's a focus to his expression as Brielle's whole body shakes, and I'm entirely in awe of the two of them. I'm happily surprised when Brielle's scream echoes so loudly, as her body comes hard. She squirts all over Judah's hand, over his thigh, and the floor beneath her is now soaked in her release.

"Fuck," she moans as her head droops forward. She looks utterly exhausted and that was only three orgasms. I can't wait for her to finally call time on this because I'm dying to feel her come on my cock.

Kai steps forward, and he stops in front of Brielle. The hiss of his zipper echoes through the room. He slowly grips his shaft, and he exposes himself to us. The way his fingers stroke up and down his length has me aching.

"I think our princess is ready to get stretched," he says, keeping his watchful gaze on her. "Aren't you, sweetheart?"

"Kai," Brielle whispers his name, but she doesn't stop him. Slowly, he inches into her. She's so wet, he slips in easily, and soon, he's fully seated inside her. Judah looks over at me, and he crooks his finger. I'm so close to them, I can smell the sex drifting in the air. I lean in to kiss Judah. His hands are at my zipper, the same way I'm at his.

We free each other's cocks, both hard, both weeping with desire. I stroke him slowly, feeling every silken inch. The wetness of his pre-cum coats my fingers, and I smile. He's more than fucking sexy, and watching the expression on his face when I pleasure him only seems to make me throb harder. The need taking over me and I'm going to need to come soon.

"I want all of you again," Brielle finally says. We stop all movement, and look over at her. "Please."

It doesn't take us long to uncuff her from the cross, and Kai settles onto a leather sofa that's sitting in the corner of the room. Brielle straddles him easily, and once again, he's deep in her pretty cunt.

It's Judah who kneels behind her this time, and I'm at the perfect height for those pretty lips to wrap around my shaft. But I'm not ready for the wet heat, and I hiss as bliss sinks under my skin, it races through my veins as Brielle takes me into her mouth, and she sucks me right up until I feel the back of her throat.

It's at that moment, Judah slides into her tight little arse, and it causes her to moan which sends vibrations through my shaft. I almost come immediately, but I fight it back for as long as I can. We move in sync. All three of us, sliding inside her. The woman we love is taking us as if she was born to become ours one day.

She was made for us.

There is no fucking doubt in my mind anymore.

We fuck, deeply, slowly, and we all seem to have the same idea in mind. We're savouring this moment because it's taken us out of the real world and thrown us into the depths of the shadows where we live.

My legs are shaking because I'm fighting to stop myself from coming, but I know I'm not going to last long. Kai captures Brielle's nipple in his mouth, and I watch as he bites down as his other hand disappears between them which causes a soft moan of pleasure to once more vibrate through my dick.

"Come for us, princess," Judah coaxes as he slams into her which only pushes her deeper onto my cock. And suddenly, we all still. Euphoria zings in my veins. My nervous system feels as if I've been electrocuted as I empty myself in Brielle's mouth. She swallows back what she can, but when I slip from her mouth, it's her and Kai who kiss, sharing the drops of seed that's coating her mouth.

We're hot breaths and moans as we slowly come down from a high I wasn't expecting. When we arrived home, the last thing on my mind was sex. But this was something else. I don't know what to call it, but it was bliss.

"You're incredible," I tell Brielle with a smile when she opens her eyes and looks up at me.

We move effortlessly to help her up, and I can tell she's tired now. Exhausted by the number of orgasms, but I know she could have taken more.

Perhaps one day we can try again. The four of us will more than likely be using this room more often from now on.

And when I scoop her up in my arms, she rests her head on my shoulder. We all make our way up to the main bedroom which has been created specifically with space for us. Having four people in a relationship means there needs to be a far bigger bed than usual.

The sky outside is dark as we settle into bed. Even a shower is out of the question for our girl right now. The moment her head hits the pillow, there are soft, peaceful snores coming from her.

A BROTHER'S GOODBYE

JUDAH

THE WEEK HAS BEEN a long one. Since Brielle's father has now been taken care of, I noticed there's a difference to her. She's changed. What she did couldn't have been easy. He's behind bars, and he's not getting out anytime soon.

Sighing as I sit back, I push the folders out of the way because my focus is not on anything I've been reading. Instead, I'm thinking about my upcoming talk with Jordan. He's finishing school in a few months, and he has to decide what he wants to do. I would much prefer he stays on Black Hollow, but I can't hold him back. I'm not going to be like my father. He ensured we would always be in this life, but if Jordan wants to venture out and do his own thing, I'll respect that.

When the office door opens, my brother walks in, and I offer him a smile. He's only a few years younger than me, and I know Dad would have been proud of him. He'll graduate with a perfect academic record.

"Having a good day, Brother?" Jordan asks as he settles back into the chair. There's a grin on his face, and I wonder just what he's got planned.

"Not exactly a busy one," I tell him. "Have you thought about what you're going to be doing after you graduate?" I steeple my fingers under my chin, and regard my brother.

"Well," he starts. "I'm going back to the mainland, I want to stay in Sicily for a while." I wasn't expecting that because he's never *left* the island long enough to show any inclination of living away from Black Hollow.

"And you'll still work for me?" I throw out the question that's been on my mind. We're blood, and I'm not going to let him just leave the organisation completely.

Jordan nods slowly. "I'm not leaving," he admits with a tip of his head. "Dad would roll around in his grave if I asked to be let go from the organisation. But, I want to work from the mainland for as long as I can. I'd like to train with The Agency."

Dad put together The Agency a long time ago. They help us when we need jobs done, but I never thought about Jordan working with them.

"You'll end up doing the dirty work," I throw back, a chuckle vibrates in my chest.

"And I don't do the dirty work here?" he challenges, this time with a grin of mischief. "You know what I mean."

"You'll start at the bottom. They're not going to give you a top rank because of your name."

Jordan shrugs it off as if he knew that bit of information already. "It doesn't bother me. Dad taught us about hard work, and I'm not at all afraid of that."

"Good. We'll miss you here."

"There's another thing," Jordan says as he leans forward, elbows on his knees. "Emilio wants to leave with me."

I arch a brow in intrigue at this bit of information. "Oh?"

"He will talk to you, but we've had a discussion about moving and he showed interest in perhaps working with The Agency as well." Jordan rests his right ankle on his left knee, and leans back to regard me.

"Then he can leave. I'm not holding anyone back,"

I tell him. "I'm not going to become one of those arseholes who keeps people from finding their true potential. If you find that you're happier with a place like The Agency, then I'll support you."

My brother's happiness means everything to me. I want him to find his passion. And I want him to fall in love. I almost laugh out loud when the thought pops into my head. It's not something I would have considered, but now that I have Brielle, things have changed. I'm even thinking about a family.

"Is that you wondering about a future for me?" Jordan asks with a sly grin on his face.

"I'm just thinking about how things have changed in the past few months. It's almost a year since Brielle was given to me and I didn't think I would understand why Dad did it."

"And you do now?" my brother murmurs as he looks at me. We've always been close. Even with the small age gap, I never thought about him as a *younger* brother. We have always been on a similar wavelength. And it's something that I've cherished. Family has been my focus for so long. The idea of me being a father though, that has emotion twisting in my chest.

"I still don't *understand* why he did it, but I know that it's for the best. She's changed me in ways I never thought about. Right now, all I want is to have children, to raise them in this world and see them grow and mature into men who can take our places one day."

"As long as you don't go getting yourself into trouble and leaving me with all this," Jordan says as he waves his hand around the room. If something were to happen to me, he would be the one to step up and lead the family.

"You know you're stuck with me until we're both old and fucking grey, Brother," I tell him with a chuckle. "Now, go, and I'll see you soon. Take the plane, make sure to send it back because I want to take Brielle to New York for the holidays."

"Take care of her, Jude," Jordan says as he rises to full height. "And I'll be back soon enough. You know I can't resist a good party on the island."

I push to my feet and round the desk. Pulling Jordan into a hug, I hold him for a long while, and I can't help but be proud of the man he's becoming.

Opening the folder with all my brother's information, I scan through the details, and I smile. My father didn't think he would ever walk away from this life, and now that he's wanting to delve deeper, I wonder if my brother knew what his choice would be.

The door opens slowly, and when I see Brielle walk in, I smile. She looks like a different person. My queen. The softness of her skin glows as she walks into the room as if she owns it. And I suppose she does. Half and half.

"I was thinking about talking to Emilio." She doesn't wait for me to say anything as she settles into the chair opposite my desk and crosses her legs. She's immaculate in a dark green knee-length dress. Her heels match her outfit and her dark hair hangs down to the middle of her back.

"I think that would be a good idea," I say to her. "I've just sat with Jordan," I continue quickly. "He wants to go and work with The Agency."

"Isn't that the company your father used for—"

"Yeah," I say before she can finish. Even though I'm still worried about him joining them, Jordan is a good fighter. "I think he'll enjoy it. There is a part of my brother who enjoys the fight. He likes to be deep in the shit which only sets me on edge. But, I have to accept it."

Brielle smiles. "You're a good brother."

"I'm an even better husband," I throw back easily.

This time, she laughs, and I find I enjoy the sound of it. "I never doubted you." Her words may be light-hearted, but there's a confession in them. I want so badly to take her right here. Even though she belongs to the three of us, I want to see her pregnant. As soon as fucking possible.

"Well," I say softly. "There were times I'm pretty sure you didn't want me to be your husband." The confession I offer her is one of brutal honesty. I know for a fact Brielle hated me when we first met. I don't blame her for her feelings, I had them too.

She lifts her hand and wiggles her fingers. The ring I put there only a week ago, shimmers in the light streaming through my office window.

"I didn't," Brielle admits. "There were moments I wanted to run, but the more you challenged me, the more Valen accepted me, and the more Kai taught me, I realised I was home."

I tip my head to the side, my gaze locking on hers. "So you're finally in acceptance?"

"I was the moment I said *I Do,* but then again, if I think about it, I know I was yours, Kai's, and Valen's, since the first night I laid eyes on you. I may have hated you," she admits with a gentle giggle. "But, you've won me over, even though you can be an arsehole at times."

This makes me laugh out loud, and I lean back. "I'm an arsehole with an amazing dick, which is why you agreed to marry me," I throw out at her with a wink.

Watching her roll her eyes makes me smile because I know our road may not have been easy, but it's perfect for us. This is how we were meant to be.

"It seems my father knew all this shit was going to work out." I don't know how he did, but he was an intelligent man. He chose this girl for me. She's challenged me since the first day I met her, and I know it won't stop until the day I take my last breath. But I also know she'll do anything for me. As I would do anything for her.

"I know when I married you, it wasn't only you I had promised myself to," Brielle admits with a soft smile. "And I'm not running away, not any time soon, or any time in the future. This is where I belong. And no matter what, our family will be ours to cherish."

"You know I want to fill that pretty little womb with my seed as soon as possible," I tell her. It's a brutal honest truth. "I've opened more than my heart to you, Brielle."

She nods slowly. "I know. I've seen your soul for a long while now, Judah. You may think you're a cold-hearted bastard, but you're not. You're more than that and you just don't like people knowing it."

"Emotions make us weak, little spy," I tell her with a shake of my head. "It's what I grew up knowing, learning, and believing."

I realise how our families are vastly different. There aren't any similarities even though we're both from the same world. Both our father's are, or at least, were, in charge of running their own organisations. Her dad walked away, while mine was killed because he was one of the most feared men in the world.

"Emotions are what make us strong," Brielle tells me. "You know why?"

I shake my head because I want to hear what she has to say. She intrigues me so much, I want to listen to her speak all day, every fucking day of my life. And I smile because I know she's mine, I know that I'll be able to learn from her until I'm old and grey.

She looks at me with a soft smile. There's a gentle crease in her expression, one that makes me think she's about to stump me with some profound wisdom. And then, she leans forward and holds my stare.

"Because when you know, when you believe, there is something worth dying for, you'll fight harder." Her voice is confident and raspy, just like I've come to learn it's a sound I love. I want to listen to it every day. And I know the rest of the guys feel the same.

"Maybe," I say as I offer a nod. "But it also shows weakness because if our enemies know you mean something to us, they can use you as collateral."

"Perhaps, but I'm a big girl, and I have three of you to watch over me like I'm a possession," Brielle throws back with a soft laugh and I know she's joking around.

"You do," I agree with a nod. "I think you should sit with Emilio. Talk to him and smooth things out."

"Why do you say it like that?"

"He's going to be leaving the island. Jordan and Emilio will be heading for The Agency, and I think it will be good for them." I pick up the folder that I was scanning earlier and I set it out for her. "This is information on The Agency, what they do for us. Since you're part of the organisation now, you should do some research and learn all there is to know."

Brielle smiles. "I want to become more invested and learn how things run, but I also don't want to take anything away from you."

"I mean, you could just stay home and have my babies," I say as I lean forward and offer her a wink.

Brielle laughs out loud. "Oh, you'd just love that. Wouldn't you?"

Shrugging, I reply, "Well, I can't deny the idea has crossed my mind a couple of times in the past few weeks. I didn't think I would ever want a family, but things have changed."

"One day," Brielle promises as she pushes to her feet. "But I want to finish school. I want to work for the organisation."

"Well, then your wish will be granted, Mrs Venier." This time, I push to my feet and head toward her. Offering her my hand, I pull her into my arms and wrap her in them.

"Go to Emilio, and we'll all have dinner later."

She leans up on her tiptoes and smiles. "I will," she promises. "Now you need to work. I don't want to be blamed if you don't get things done."

I lean in closer, stealing her lips with mine, and I can't stop the moan of pleasure that rumbles in my chest. She makes me happy. And I know the guys love her just as much. Kai and Valen have come to need her in their lives as much as I love her. That's the important part of this dynamic, it has to work for us all, or it won't work.

I didn't expect her. She appeared one day and now I don't want her to leave. She's burrowed herself so deeply into my life, into our lives, I can't imagine the future without her anymore.

"Now go," I say when I reluctantly break the kiss and step back, allowing my hands to drop to my sides. If I hold onto her for any longer, I will be tempted to take her right here in my office.

Brielle just smiles as she walks out of the office. Watching her leave, I shake my head at the sway of her hips. I know what she's doing. But she's right, I have to work.

But tonight, we'll spend the evening together, all four of us.

THERE ARE moments in your life you don't truly think about. Things happen, and you move on. All my life, I was taught to focus on what's coming, rather than what has been. My father made sure to give me enough answers to appease me, but he never confessed the whole truth. Not until I was face-to-face with him.

He isn't the man I thought he was. And now, I'm sitting across from my half-brother. We're both innocent in this, and I still can't believe I've found a home, and a family, one I didn't even know I had here in Black Hollow.

It was a good idea for me to sit with Emilio. It's still difficult to call him that because it is Dad's name. But he's nothing like our father. When I look into his eyes, he may resemble the man somewhat, but his soul isn't tarnished, not in the way our father's was.

"I wasn't sure we'd ever get this chance, not before I left anyway," Emilio says as he sits back on the sofa, holding the coffee cup in his hands.

"When I saw him it hit me that I can't blame you, or be angry with you. We both didn't know that the other existed, and watching how easy it is to lose someone, I don't want us to go through that."

"Family is important," Emilio says with a nod of agreement. "I didn't know our father very well. I only ever saw him once, and that was just before you both disappeared. I was brought here, and deep down, I figured it was the end of the road for him. I honestly didn't think he would have survived as long as he has."

"Now that I know everything, I realise how out of the loop I've been with everything around me." I sip my own coffee, and close my eyes when the warmth of it calms me. When I look at Emilio again, I say, "I hope that we can build a relationship. I don't want to be someone you avoid for any reason. I know things aren't always easy, but I am here for you."

"Hey," he says while gifting me a smile. "I'm not going to be running off anytime soon. I do want to train with The Agency though. Their work fascinates me, but also, I know that it's something I need to do to work through the stress of the past few months."

I understand what he means. There's been so much emotion, so many fires to put out, I know exactly what it feels like to have your world thrown upside down.

"Well, you'll always have a home to come to here on Black Hollow. And once I graduate, I'm going to be working alongside Judah. It will give me an opportunity to see things first-hand."

"Are you sure you want to do that?" The concern in Emilio's eyes makes me smile. He cares about me and my well-being which fills my heart with joy. When we first met, I was convinced I would never accept him as my brother. But times change, things have progressed, and now I can't imagine him anywhere else.

I ponder his question for a moment. I could do anything I wanted to and I know Jude would accept and support me, but I promised to be by his side, and if I'm honest with myself, I do want to learn about the organisation. I want to know how it runs, I want to train with the rest of the soldiers. Perhaps not in combat, yet, but I am ready for a new challenge.

"I do." I nod then. "I've thought about it, and when I posed the idea to Judah, he said he would support me in anything I'd like to do. And now that I'm able to put my skills to the test, both academic and physical, I want to go all in. I doubt I could work in a place like The Agency, killing isn't my strong suit, but I do like the undercover work."

"It will put you in danger." It's a warning, one that I know all too well. I didn't want to be in this life for such a long time, and now I can't picture myself leading any semblance of what people would think is a normal life.

"I know, there are times I wonder if I'm sane when I consider my decision, but"—I pause as I set the cup down and push to my feet—"I'll have the biggest and meanest bodyguards watching over me, and when you're home, you'll be here too. I won't ever put myself in any necessary danger. I can promise you that."

"She definitely won't," Jordan says as he walks into the room. "My brother will more than likely lock her in the basement if she even so much as thinks about doing something stupid."

"And I wouldn't blame Judah for it either," Emilio throws out with a chuckle, and I can't stop myself from lobbing a cushion at his head. Both guys laugh.

"What violence is going on in here?" Judah questions when he saunters into the living room. He makes his way straight to me, and not long after he's entered, Valen and Kai join us.

We truly are a family. One I'm more than proud to be a part of. I can't imagine my life without them now.

"Emilio was just saying how he'd help you lock me in the basement if I tried to put myself in any danger." I look at Judah who's nodding, offering a wink to me, but he grins at my brother.

"Trust me, mate," he says then. "She'll have three of us to contend with. She's strong, but not that strong. We'll make sure she's alive and well."

"You guys do know I'm standing right here," I retort as I pout at my husband, and then the rest of the guys who are now laughing loudly.

"We better head off before Brielle locks us all up in the damn basement," Jordan announces and he looks over to where Emilio is. They're leaving tonight, and I already feel the pang of heartbreak at seeing my brother leave. We only just got to know each other, and now, he's heading off. I know it will be good for him, but I'll miss him, and that's what's so difficult to handle.

Emilio comes to me first, before he goes to any of

the guys. He pulls me into a hug and I allow myself to let go of all the stress that's held me back in the past few months. Even though I've let Judah, Kai, and Valen in, there's something different about my brother. He's my blood, and I'm happy that we've managed to ease the tension between us.

"I hope to be back for your graduation," Emilio whispers in my ear, making me smile. "I'll be sure to message you when and if I can. There may be limits on the amount of outside contact, but I'll always be here for you. From now until the end," he promises and I hug him tighter, not wanting to consider the fact that there could be danger he's walking into. It's stupid, because our lives are filled with danger, but I can't think about it, or I will break down and cry.

We pull away from each other, and he looks into my eyes. He reminds me so much of Papa, but also, he's unique in his own right.

"Look after yourself," he says with a smile before he heads off to say goodbye to the rest of the guys.

When Jordan pulls me in for a hug, he holds me tight for a long, silent moment and then he steps back. His hands grip my shoulders, and he meets my eyes. It's what I imagine looking at Judah when he was younger would have been like. The same, naughty smirk, the flicker of mischief in his eyes. And just as devastatingly handsome.

"Look after my brother, I know he's an asshole at times, but he's a good guy under that tough exterior." It's the first time we've spoken so openly. We have joked around, but nothing that equals this.

Nodding, I smile. "I'll always look after him. I'll look after them," I add, knowing that I have a responsibility not only to my husband, but to the other two men who love me too.

"I know you will," Jordan offers before he and Emilio wave a goodbye from the waiting car. It's a bittersweet goodbye, because I wanted to spend more time with them. Both of them. Even though Jordan isn't my blood relation, he is now part of an extended family I've inherited.

It feels good to belong somewhere. All my life, I was afraid of what would happen if Papa ever got caught. He was always careful, but there are no guarantees in life. Deep down, I always wondered if when I got home from school I'd find him gone, or worse. But he was always there, waiting on me.

"Was it good to talk to Emilio?" Judah asks as we make our way back to the living room and settle on the sofas. I'm exhausted, but I'm happy. It's almost a foreign feeling to me as I consider months ago I thought my life was over.

"Yeah." I nod as I recall our chat. It wasn't long, but it was enough to know we're family. "I just wish they didn't have to leave so soon. But I also understand, life needs to move on."

"Speaking of," Judah says. "Jordan wanted to stay, but they had to start their training. But, the ceremony is tomorrow." It's a reminder of who we're about to be. Stepping into roles I would have said we're far too young for, but the world we come from is welcoming us with open arms.

"Are you ready?" I ask him. What's also happening on Saturday is Judah's birthday. September twenty-nine. The day he's probably looked forward to all his life.

"I think I was born ready," he tells us.

"I know the moment I'm walking into the room to do mine, I'll just want the shit to be over. It's a long, tedious process, and it could take all day." Valen sighs as he pushes to his feet and heads for the liquor cabinet. "Drinks?"

"Scotch for me," Judah says.

"Me too," Kai orders.

Valen looks to me and I ponder for a moment before asking, "Can I have a white wine please?" I know there's an open bottle in the bar fridge right next to him, so he doesn't have to go to the kitchen for it.

"It's too fucking quiet," Kai grumbles before picking up the remote and turning on the sound system. The heavy bass vibrates through the room and he fiddles with the buttons until it's at a listening volume and the song streams through the surrounding speakers.

"This feels so strange," I say suddenly as I consider that we're just sitting around. There are no threats that we know about. We're not looking for anyone, and we don't have to be anywhere right now.

"What does?" Valen asks as he settles opposite me on the large sofa and rests his feet on Kai's lap.

Shrugging, I look at each of them and say, "I don't know. It's so quiet. There's a calmness to this evening. One I definitely didn't expect. Especially since we still have three large ceremonies to attend. I mean, you're all three about to take over organisations that have been around for thousands of years."

The guys are silent for a long while before Judah speaks, "That's true, but they're also roles we've all been playing for a few years now. I've been running my father's company since he died, and Valen has had to oversee a lot of agreements since his mother can't do it. And Kai's had to accompany Mario to quite a few different meetings with their contacts."

He's right. "I suppose so," I whisper. "I still find that the quiet is too much for me. I almost expect a hundred men to burst through the doors and start shooting again."

"Don't jinx it, princess," Kai throws out before he swallows back his drink and looks over to Valen for a refill.

"I don't mean to, honestly. Perhaps I'm just so used to something going on, that the calm is strange."

"I mean," Valen adds as he waggles his eyebrows. "There are loads of games we can play," he says.

"Is sex the only thing you think about?" This comes from an exasperated Judah who makes me laugh.

"I mean, not always," Valen shrugs, then pouts as he gets the bottle of whisky from the cabinet, and settles back into his position on the sofa.

"I think we should settle in the home cinema and watch a movie," Kai says, surprising me. "What?" He looks at me with a grin. "I do normal things too."

"Ha," my laugh bounces off the walls as the music

dies as the sound falls from my lips. "What would you like to watch then?"

He ponders for a moment before he says, "We can watch one of the classics like Dracula, or something scary."

I'm shaking my head before he has time to finish what he's saying. "No scary movies. How about something lighter, or perhaps action?"

In unison, as if they are reading each other's minds, all three men say, "Fast and the Furious franchise."

I can't help but groan, but then again, I can't deny there is some delicious eye candy in those movies. I nod. "Fine."

"You know there are now ten movies out?" Val challenges as we all move from the living room to the cinema. I didn't even know this room existed. It's darkened with blackout curtains and comfortable lounge seats which are soft velvet. The screen is pretty much the size it would be in a normal movie house.

"This is amazing."

"And it's all ours," Judah says as he pulls me down to sit beside him, and Kai and Valen snuggle in beside me. When Jude picks up a phone on the arm rest, he orders, "Can you bring some popcorn and drinks down for us. Just a selection of whatever is chilled."

It doesn't take long for one of the staff who I usually see working in the kitchen to make her way down to where we're seated. A small trolley is filled with three buckets of popcorn, bags of sweets, and I note there are doors at the bottom of the silver tray and when they're opened, there is a selection of wine, beer, and some cider.

This is nothing like I've experienced before. My own personal cinema, along with three of the most beautiful men in the world.

I am a lucky girl.

A CEREMONY

JUDAH

I open my eyes to the darkness outside. The sun hasn't risen yet, and when I push off the bed, careful not to wake anyone else still asleep, I pad silently over to the balcony. I should go downstairs and make coffee, but I realise that I'm nervous.

It's been the same emotion within a few days, and now it's back and I don't know how to deal with it. This isn't like the wedding. When I married Brielle, it was easier than the idea of what I'm going to go through today.

I recall the day I stepped up from Capo. My father ensured I went through the due process. I didn't skip anything because I was his son.

All my life, I've waited for this moment. The day I wake up on my twenty-fifth birthday, and I gain some form of independence, but I also inherit a world that will answer to me. A family, a clan, an organisation.

I don't expect it to be easy today. It will be exhausting because I'll have to answer to the men who worked with my father all his life.

They're not going to take it easy on me and I don't want them to. I should be treated like every other upcoming Boss there is and I will make it through.

Granted, there are vows and promises to recite, there's blood to be spilled, and there is a contract that I will have to sign in the crimson that drips from my hand. The ceremony may only last the day, but the clan is there forever. And in a few weeks, Jordan will have to return to Black Hollow to step up into the Underboss position. He will have to go through all this bullshit like I did.

I inhale the early morning air, it's fresh, and I close my eyes and focus on the silence. The only sound that fills my senses are the waves crashing against the cliff. The mansion overlooks the ocean, and each day I look out at the view, I thank God I'm able to see it.

I feel her before I hear her. She's behind me, and I wonder briefly if she's going to try to surprise me.

But I can't stop myself from saying, "Good morning."

"You're no fun," Brielle pouts. I can hear the expression in her tone. She makes me chuckle when she does that because I find it so alluring, I want to drag her back to bed and show her just how fun I can be.

Turning on my heel, I open my arms to her and she snuggles into my chest.

"I wanted to wake you with something special," she murmurs into my bare skin, then tilts her head to look up at me.

"Oh?" This has me rather intrigued.

"Well," she starts shyly, "It's your birthday, and you should be enjoying the morning in bed."

"Is that right?" I ask her as I lean in to steal her lips with mine. "I think you should drag me back inside then."

A soft giggle vibrates in her chest, and she takes my hand and leads me into the bedroom where I find Kai and Valen waiting. They're both naked from the waist up, but from the way the sheets are draped over them, there's more happening that I can't see quite yet.

"Join us," Kai invites me and I can't deny the prospect of spending the day in bed with the three loves of my life sounds like a lot more fun than work. But I also can't be late.

"Lie back," Brielle orders, and the three of us exchange a look of confusion. She rushes to the stereo and turns on the sound system that fills the room with a soft, seductive tune.

And then, she dances for us. Her hips sway as she slowly undresses. She strips out of the short nightdress she'd been draped in, and soon, she's naked on the bed. I watch her crawl toward me, and that's when Kai and Valen shift and soon, I'm the centre of attention.

This is definitely the way a king should spend his birthday. They kiss and lick every inch of me, and when Valen and Brielle lean in and stroke my cock with their mouths on either side, I almost lose all control.

Kai moves up to my mouth, and he presses his lips to mine. The way his tongue sweeps along mine has my blood burning and my cock throbbing. I am so close. I can so easily come, but I hold back for a moment longer, savouring every moment.

Either Valen or Brielle cup my balls, and they give them a squeeze which sends me right over the fucking edge. When Kai pulls away, he kneels beside me on the mattress, and Brielle leans forward to kiss him. The slickness of my release still painted on her lips, and on her cheek. Watching Kai and Valen, and my wife kiss and lick at the wetness has me wondering if I can cancel the ceremony tonight and spend all the fucking hours I have in this bed with them. Because this is the hottest scene I have ever witnessed in my life.

When they look over at me, they offer me their biggest smiles and say, "Happy Birthday, Judah."

"Well, I have to say, I've had some interesting birthdays in my past, and I have had celebrations that I thought were great, but that..." My words filter off into silence because I don't have any way of describing how I feel right now.

"And next up, Kai and me are making you breakfast," Valen announces. "Brielle will keep you company because you're not allowed downstairs, and you're not allowed to be alone at all today."

When the guys leave, I know what they're doing. I know why Brielle stayed back. She wants to talk. The look on her face tells me everything as she settles on the mattress, and tugs the sheet to cover her breasts.

"What's on your mind?"

She looks at me in surprise when I ask her, and she smiles. "I wanted to hear how you're feeling about today. It's a big step, and it can't be easy, especially when it's on a day you should be relaxing with friends and enjoying the down time from work."

She's right, but I learned from my father there aren't any days off. And then again, he worked himself into an early grave. Perhaps I shouldn't follow all the things he's taught me.

"I'm scared I'm not going to live up to everyone's expectations of how I should be," I blurt out suddenly. It's been playing on my mind for a few weeks now. Even though I've been wanting to run the organisation all my life, there is still a lot of pressure that comes with the role.

Brielle shifts and kneels on the bed, the sheet now forgotten. She cups my face in her hands, it's a gentle touch, and it slows my racing heart rate.

"You are the man your father raised. You're good, you're strong, and you know what you're doing. And if you find yourself at a loss, you have me, Kai, and Valen."

I don't know how my father knew her so well to choose her for me, but he was right. "You know, the letter he wrote me said he knew you would be good for me."

Brielle laughs softly. "He said the same thing to me."

"I guess, even in his weakest moments, my father knew how to do this."

"And so will you," Brielle reassures me, and I push back all those doubts that have sprung to the surface. I need to trust in me, and our family, and I need to trust in my father.

THE ROOM WE'RE USHERED INTO IS DARK, ONLY LIT BY the candelabra hanging from the centre of the circular space. There are also smaller pillar lamps that dance with a live flame.

Each man surrounding the table is dressed in all black. The same as myself, Kai, and Valen. While Brielle is in a dark grey dress, her long flowing hair hangs straight down to the middle of her back. It looks like we're heading to a funeral.

"Judah Venier," a deep rumble comes from one of the older men in the room. His hair is a full head of salt, with small strands of pepper. "Welcome to your initiation ceremony."

"Thank you." I'm not sure what to say, or do. He then

crooks his finger and calls me over to the head of the table. On the large wooden surface, I spy the contract I will be signing, and the oath of Omertà, which I've already taken, but this is for a whole new position.

Also on the table, beside the old vellum pages that look like they come from old Roman times, is the dagger, and beside it, the gun. The blade is one I'll use to cut my hand and bleed my allegiance to the clan. And to the mafia.

"Everyone, be seated," the announcement comes and this morning's distraction is a long gone memory now. I'm a deer caught in headlights. Even though I've been through something similar when I took the role of Underboss, I know this will hold so much more responsibility.

"Tonight, we welcome the eldest son of the Venier clan. He's been a force to be reckoned with so far in his job as the Underboss to his father. But, tragedy struck and now, he's going to be taking the helm."

Another of the older men rises to his feet, and he says, "Tonight, the Prince will become a King. And beside him, the Queen will also rise to power. The decision has been made that she will rule with her husband, rather than take a back seat in the organisation."

"Will Brielle Venier please rise, and join us at the head of the table." My head snaps up and I look over at my wife. We didn't expect this. She wasn't meant to be a part of this, but with confidence, she squares her shoulders and rises to full height.

"Thank you," Brielle says with a slight curtsy before she makes her way toward me. We're standing at the front of the room, at least, what I would call it as it's circular in shape. But the large, ornate chair that represents the King's seat is right before me.

"Firstly, we will ask Judah to take the blade, and press it to his palm, as he recites the oath." The older man gestures for me to continue, and I know I have no choice. Not that I want one, but I'm still fucking nervous.

I obey the elder and as the blood drips from my hand, I utter the words, "My blood means that we are now one Family, and I take the seat at the top. I am now King of the Venier clan. I live by the gun and the knife and I will die by the gun and the knife."

Those silver eyes that were piercing through me land on Brielle. "And now, it's your turn."

I don't want to see her bleed. But Brielle is strong. She takes the blade from my hand, and she presses it to her palm, mimicking what I did. And when her crimson life force drips onto mine on the paper, she says, "My blood means that we are now one Family, and I take the seat at the top. I am now Queen of the Venier clan. I live by the gun and the knife and I will die by the gun and the knife."

Even though I know it's an oath she has to voice, the idea of her dying makes my gut churn. She can't leave me with this shitstorm that we're taking over. I need her by my side. I'm surprised at my thoughts once more.

"We will now sign the contract using the blood from you both," the elder announces. Even though this was the easy part, the dinner after will be long and tedious. We will have to meet each of the men in this room. We will have to answer questions and hopefully appease their concerns. We're young, much younger than most of the men who are currently running their own clans. But I know we can be better at it.

Once our signatures are dried on the vellum, the contract is rolled up and it's bound with a bright red ribbon. It will forever be stored in the archives. And when our children one day take over, they will then see what we did when we were the ones standing here.

We're given cloth bandages to wrap around our

hands, and a pin each to secure them in place. I want to laugh, but I don't disrespect the elders who are here.

It's still crazy for me to think about, knowing my Dad was one of the men who signed his life away to an organisation he ran for more than forty years. He was a few years younger than I am today when he took over, and yet, he did it with the confidence that made it seem as if he was born with the dagger in his hand.

It takes a few long moments for the rest of the men to file out, and for the contracts to be stored. By the time we're welcomed into the dining hall, I am ready to go to bed. I'm surprised when I walk in with Brielle's hand in mine, to find there's a birthday cake waiting on me.

"We wanted to wish you a proper happy birthday," Giacomo says, and I recognise him as one of Dad's most trusted allies. He's been running his organisation for as long as I can remember, and probably far longer as he's almost eighty now. "Your father would have been so proud to see his eldest up there taking the oath."

"Well, I appreciate that. He did watch me as I took the Underboss and the Capo initiation vows."

He probably doesn't remember, but as I say the words, he slowly nods.

"Oh, right," he says then. "I'm an old man, Judah. One day, when you're like me, you'll be lucky because you have a beautiful wife to keep you young." He guffaws, for an older man it's a booming sound. "It's lovely to meet you, sweetheart."

He holds out a hand to Brielle who accepts without a second guess. "And you, Mr—"

"Oh, call me Giacomo," he tells her. "Everybody and their donkey does."

"Well, I do hope you don't hear donkey's talking, they say it's a sign you're getting old." There's a soft giggle from Brielle, but once again, it's Giacomo's laugh that bounces around the room calling attention to us at the one end of the table.

"I like you, young lady," he tells my wife. "You've got a good one there, Judah." I've been told.

"Oh, I know. Now all I can do is pray she keeps me around." This time, there's a few more people who join in on the jovial chat, and I relax into the evening.

I realise as I sit and talk to the men who have been in this world for longer than I've been alive, tomorrow a whole new role opens up to me. With every laugh, and every joke, I look over at Kai and

Valen as they enjoy their moments with some of the men and women who are in attendance, and I know they'll soon be in my shoes too.

We're all grown up.

And we're going to rule the fucking world.

THE FUTURE IS BRIGHT

BRIELLE

One Year Later

THE BABIES ARE KICKING as I lie back on the sofa. Twins. Two of them growing inside me. It's still surreal when I feel them move.

My focus has been nothing short of frustrating. All I can think of is making sure I have the nursery ready, but since I'm not allowed to do anything, I can't go up and check that the guys are actually listening to my demands. I've become one of those nightmare wives, ordering each of my men around like they're servants. But then again, if they didn't like it, they should allow me to see what's being done in the room.

I wanted to make sure I was happy with the colours, and to oversee the painting, furnishings, and the mobiles that will hang over each of the cribs. Everything has to be perfect.

I wonder if my mother was like this when she knew she was pregnant with me. Deep down, I feel an emptiness when I have quiet moments, it overtakes me and it reminds me that I don't have a mother figure to ask.

But, I know I've overcome so many things, I can get through this with the support of all three of my men. They're like bodyguards, watching over me. I'm never alone at home, thankfully, and when I'm at school, they have the soldiers who are working their way to Capos guarding me as if I'm a prized possession.

Before I got pregnant, I trained with Kai every day though. I didn't want to feel uneasy if I were ever put in a situation where I needed to defend myself. Judah agreed, and the training I started when I first arrived, advanced, and just before they all forbid me to do anything too strenuous, I was doing well.

But having two babies inside me, kicking non-stop lately, I don't have any inclination to do anything physical. Even sex has slowed down. I don't *feel* sexy, even though Judah, Kai, and Valen have fought me tooth and nail on the fact. They're still trying to convince me I look even sexier now than I did before.

I don't believe them.

Sighing, I push to my feet, and slowly move toward the windows. There are gardeners outside working on the flowerbeds. Two summer born babies are coming and everything has to be perfect for their arrival. I know why though, we'll have the whole organisation here. All the elders will want to see the children, and welcome them into the clan.

There are so many rituals and ceremonies that come with being in the mafia, and so many rules to follow, it can be exhausting at times. But, I can safely say, so far I'm getting used to it.

I glance down at the ring on my fingers with fondness. I didn't think I wanted to love him when I first saw him, but my heart knew better.

I close my eyes and recall the day I walked into the lawyer's office. My father introduced me, and I was a mix of emotions. Hate, anger, frustration, but there was also desire. There was no denying it because Judah Venier is more than handsome.

Even then I didn't want to admit how much I craved him. Each time we fought, argued, or bickered, every moment he was close to me, I ached.

But that wasn't the end of it. When I walked into the Venier mansion and I saw Kai and Valen, something inside me had clicked into overdrive. I thought perhaps I had just not had enough sex before arriving at the island, but it was just fate toying with my future.

I was thrown into the lion's den, and there was no getting out. I didn't want to escape after a while. Now, I know I was brought here for a reason and I am happy. I find myself more at peace now than I ever was as a child growing up.

"Are you lost in thought again," Judah joins me then. It's been a year since he took over the helm from his father, and the organisation is running perfectly. There haven't been too many issues, nobody has needed any torture, and he has only killed a small handful of enemies.

I can't believe I find that so *normal* now. Before, it would have appalled me and I would have been a mess. Now though, I know my husband is here, wanting to keep our family safe.

"I was just thinking back to the day I met you for the first time," I tell him as I press my lips to his stubbled cheek. He's got a small smattering of salt in the dark strands of his hair which makes me smile. He's getting older, maturing, and just like a fine wine, I can drink him in all day.

"Oh," he says, "You mean the day you fell in love with me but hid it because you were too scared to admit how handsome you thought I was. And it was also the day you realised that your needs were far more complex than you thought they were."

"How so?"

"It was the day you came to Black Hollow, and fantasised about me, Kai, and Valen fucking you." There's a knowing smile on his lips, and I realised he must have seen me that night. The warmth that heats my cheeks makes me want to shy away and hide. I can't believe he was watching me.

"You were there?" I whisper as I glance up and find the flicker of desire in his eyes.

The corner of his mouth ticks upward, the slight dip of a dimple creases in his cheek, and he nods. "I was coming to your room to tell you that dinner would be ready. I did want to make sure you ate so you could keep your strength up, but then I heard the shower, and let's just say, I'm curious."

"Far too curious for your own good," I retort, slapping him on the shoulder. "Why didn't you say anything? Or even tell me when we finally admitted our feelings?"

Judah shrugs. "I don't know. It wasn't something I wanted to use against you in any way. I wanted you to find your emotions out for yourself, but also, when I did see you, I was so angry in that moment, I didn't want to admit to myself that even then I wanted you so fiercely, I struggled with my emotions."

"You definitely did struggle in the past, but at the moment, you're not that bad. You've slowly learned how to let me in. I think perhaps you were more scared than anything else."

I wrap my arms around his waist, but there's not much room to get closer with my belly taking up the space.

"I was," Judah admits. I spent so long wanting to please everyone who I thought mattered in my life, that I didn't see who I really was. And I also didn't want Kai and Valen to be pulled into any more shit because of their lifestyle choices. For me, I didn't actually give a shit. But they mean so much to me, I couldn't put them in danger."

"I get that," I tell him. Nodding, I continue, "I didn't expect you to trust me from the first day. Hell, I didn't trust any of you. Even though Valen was friendly, and more approachable than you or Kai, even he was still kept at arm's length because I didn't know what to do with myself."

"But you held your own," Judah reminds me. "Which is probably why I knew you could handle us. You're a strong woman, little spy," he whispers against my lips before he kisses me deeply.

As much as I think I don't want sex, whenever one of them teases or taunts me, just like Judah does with his tongue right now, I can't stop my body from responding, my thighs squeezing together, and my whimpers vibrating in my chest.

"Is someone in need of some release?" Judah speaks against my lips as he flicks his tongue over the bottom one, then the top.

"Jude," Kai calls from the door, causing Judah to groan in frustration. I can't stop the giggle that escapes my mouth. "Sorry, mate, we need to head out to the school."

"Something wrong?" I ask, stepping in front of Judah.

Kai shakes his head, but he doesn't look at me when he replies, "No, just something needs dealing with."

This time, I'm moving toward Kai. I stop right in front of him, my hands at my sides, fisting to keep from shaking him because I want to know what the hell is wrong. "Which means something is wrong."

Kai's gaze drops to mine, and he meets me dead on. "Please, princess, it's nothing to do with you or us, but we need to go and see one of the professors."

"Let's go." Jude and Kai both kiss my cheeks before they head off and I'm left on my own. I didn't see Valen go with them, so I head up to his bedroom to see if he's in. I know they hardly ever leave me alone, especially now that I'm pregnant, so he should be here somewhere.

It's frustrating being left out of work, but I have to deal with it. It won't be long now and I'll have the babies. Once they're here, we can go back to a semblance of normal. I can be back at work after I take my maternity leave, but I know I won't be sitting at home forever. I'd be bored out of my mind.

"Val?" I knock on his bedroom door and wait. We all kept our respective rooms, in case we need a break from each other. Mine has been turned into a library for the most part, with my bed still against the one wall. But all my clothes are in our main bedroom which we had fitted specifically for the four of us.

"Come in, princess," Val calls to me and I step inside to find him painting. He only started recently, and I smile when I see it's of the garden. A beautiful sunset, illuminating the scene below it.

I don't wait for him to say anything before I enquire, "What's going on at the school?"

Valen sighs as he swipes the paintbrush across the canvas. "There's been an incident, but you don't need to worry about it because the guys will take care of it."

I know what he means by *take care of it* and that's what sets me on edge. "If it's something that needs Judah and Kai to sort it out then it means it's serious."

He knows I won't give this up until he tells me exactly what's happened. Valen has put up with my stubbornness for a long while now, and he's come to get used to it as well. Even when I'm being a bitch about something, he'll appease me in some way. He's different to the others, and I know that he'll be the one to keep me in the loop if ever Kai and Jude decide to take things into their own hands. Which is more often than not.

"Well," Valen says as he sets the palette down along with his paintbrushes. "There's been an attack, so they're going to interview some witnesses to get to the bottom of it."

"What attack?" My mouth pops open in shock,

and I'm immediately anxious. It's not good for the babies, but I now know why they didn't want to tell me what happened.

I should have left it. But my curious nature took over and now I'm on edge. I pace the room as Valen watches me for a quiet moment.

"Brielle," his voice draws me to him, and I stop in front of where he's perched on a high stool. "It's going to be okay. There is no need for you to worry."

"Just tell me what the attack was," I plead with him. "If I don't know, my mind plays out all these terrible scenarios and then I can't sleep or think straight."

He knows I'm right. It's just in my nature to be this way. I've never known any different. When I was younger, I would think up all these vivid details about something when I didn't get the full story. I wonder briefly if I should have become an author. Making up fantastical tales of monsters and princesses.

"I need you to stay calm, okay?" Valen takes my hands and he holds them close. His eyes are boring a hole right through me and now I know something very bad has happened. If he's taking on a serious tone, then it's terrible.

"Okay." Even though I say it, I'm not sure I can abide by my promise. The word I utter is so slow, and so soft, it's barely audible, even to me. My chest is tight, and my stomach is heavy, not with the fact that I'm carrying twins, but because I know that whatever Valen is about to admit, will shatter my heart.

And then, very slowly, Valen speaks. "One of the female students was raped."

I croak my reply, "What?"

"Jordan, Judah, and Kai are there." I forgot that my brother-in-law was visiting. He arrived back a few days ago, Emilio is still out on a job.

But the news rocks me and I open my mouth to speak, but I can't find the words.

"It's going to be sorted out, I promise. We will make sure that she gets all the help she needs, and the person responsible will be dealt with accordingly.

"When?"

"Someone came forward with a testimony from last night's party, which is why we need to keep this hush for now. Once Judah returns, we can sit down and talk."

I still have no idea what to say. It's not the first time I hear something like this happening. In the big cities, it's a daily occurrence, but it's the first time something like this is so close to home.

We all went out to the races last night. It had been a while since the guys were able to attend or take part. I don't remember anything happening, but then again, I didn't stay too long. If it happened while I was there, I would have probably seen the girl, and the perpetrator.

Suddenly, I feel sick. "I hope he gets what's coming to him," I bite out as I look up at Valen.

He offers me a dark smile. "Oh," he says, "Trust me when I say, the guys don't take lightly to something like this."

For the millionth time since I came to Black Hollow, I'm more proud to be with them than I ever have been.

I love all the men in my newfound family.

EPILOGUE

KAI

Life brings you moments of doubt, instances of fear, and whirlwinds of change. Those are things I've been through for most of my life. I didn't expect to find happiness ever. But then, when I was taken in by the Errani family, I realised that not all people are bad.

Over the years, I grew up with a family. I had parents who loved me. And I had a brother who even though it took us a while to connect, we found common ground.

What I didn't expect was to be adopted into a family that was part of the world of the mafia. It wasn't like a *normal* family. No, these were violent, ruthless bastards who didn't care what they did, as long as the job got done.

Even though it wasn't easy, I found myself. Deep down, I was at ease with my situation, it was a place I could work, I could learn, and I could grow.

All my life I needed it, and it landed in my lap as if by a miracle. I did think it was all too good to be true, but, as time went on, I realised it was real. I mean, I didn't wake up from a dream, and I certainly wasn't ripped away from this new family. I'm not sure to this day why they chose me, but I know I made it, and that's all that matters to me.

I look out of the window and watch the kids playing. Valen is chasing them while Judah is calling for them to go eat their lunch. The sun is shining, and the warmth of it bathes me as I stand on the balcony of our home.

I didn't expect to still be here, with them, four years after the wedding, after we each received our organisations to run, but I am. And I'm thankful for every fucking moment of it.

"Are you enjoying the quiet up here?" Brielle slides her arms around me and I smile. There's a warmth to her that calms all the dark and irrational thoughts in my mind.

"I was just watching our family," I tell her as we stand in the quiet, the only sounds are of giggles and squeals from below. "It's nice to see happiness."

When Brielle had the twins, we didn't know who the father was. To be honest, we didn't want to know. But we have a feeling from their eye colour, we do think it is Judah's. But in the arrangement, we may have to try again, and again.

"So, are you ready for another set of twins?" I tease as I turn to face her, and pull her close.

Brielle laughs, her head falling back as she arches into me. Then those pretty eyes meet mine. "I think perhaps we need to have a talk amongst ourselves."

Even though work has been keeping us all busy, I doubt the guys would argue if we wanted to get Brielle pregnant again. Because that would mean we would all have to spend more time in the bedroom, and less in the office.

"I'm happy," I tell her.

She nods and smiles. "You deserve to be, we all do, and our forever is only beginning."

Brielle

BEING A MOTHER HAS COME NATURALLY TO ME. I didn't think it would, but as I watch the kids race around the garden with their three dads, I can't help but feel at peace.

Work has been busy, and I've taken on teaching at the university. Black Hollow has offered me a new lease on life. But as I gently massage my growing belly with my palm, I pray that our next child will be as happy and carefree as the other two. Twins.

We finally got some tests done and found out it was Judah who was the dad. I wanted to give each of the men in my life a child, and now that I'm pregnant with Valen's baby, and we know it's only one this time, I smile because I know he's going to be incredible with our son or daughter.

Living a life that isn't what society deems *normal* has given me a new insight into how easily people are judged. It's disheartening that there are those out there who can treat each other with hatred and disrespect.

We aren't hurting anyone. We don't harm those around us, and yet, we're still gawked at when we're out. Even though people don't know the true extent of our connection, or the dynamics of our relationship, there are still close-minded individuals who think it's wrong.

But those are the people I choose to ignore. You

must be rather sad to live your life bullying and insulting others.

I love my life.

I love my men.

And nothing will ever change that.

Valen

HOLDING MY SON FOR THE FIRST TIME IS SURREAL. Looking down in those dark eyes, I see myself. I don't think I have ever felt so much love, it's overwhelming. He has my blood running through his veins. There is something deeply emotional about it.

"Hey, little guy." I look down at his scrunched up nose, and how he wraps his tiny fingers around mine. "When you're all grown up, I'm going to remind you of this moment where you made me feel like the most important person in the world."

"You are," Brielle says as she enters the gym where I'm sitting on the floor with our baby in my arms. "He's going to grow up to be just like his dad."

"Well," I say looking up at her. "As long as he shows respect and morals, then I know I've done well. I don't want him to be anything other than good. And if he doesn't want to be in this life, and he wants to carve out his own path, I won't force him into it.

"You're already a good father," Brielle whispers as she gently presses a fingertip to the tip of his nose. "Everyone is waiting on you," she says then. "We're ready for lunch."

As we both stand, and we walk out of the gym, I say to her, "Thank you for changing my life and showing me I am worthy of love." I don't know why I'm so fucking emotional, but I need her to know, she means a lot to me.

"Always," she promises and we make our way into the noisy dining room to join the rest of our family.

Judah

I HAVE NOW COME TO ACCEPT THESE *FEELINGS*.

Yes, I'm an arsehole. But my wife makes me a better man. I know I don't tell her that often enough, I'm hoping she notices it though. Watching her with the children is like watching a movie. I don't believe it's my life.

Deep down, all I can hope is that my father is looking down at me and he's proud. I spent my life waiting to hear those words from him, but even in his final letter to me, I didn't get it.

"Mr Venier," a voice from my office door has me turning to face Romeo. Yeah, his mother really named him that. "There's a parcel for you." He sets the box down on my desk and steps back.

"Thank you, you can leave." Once I'm alone, I settle into my office chair and cut the tape open with my dagger. Lifting the lid slightly, I get a whiff of perfume. Inside, are two teddy bears, both smell like talcum powder and jasmine. It's a soft, gentle fragrance.

I lift them out and I notice they're wearing tags around their necks.

Venier Baby One
Venier Baby Two

UNDER THE BEARS, IS AN ENVELOPE WITH MY NAME scrawled on the front, and once again, it's in my father's script.

Judah,

This may come as a shock to you, but I hope that it reaches you at the perfect moment. I know I'll never meet my grandchildren, so I wanted to give them something to remember me with. I want you to tell him about me, remind them of our family oath, and the beliefs I instilled in you and Jordan.

But I also want you to know, I love you. You have been my successor since you were born and with every year that passed, I watched you become a man. At first, I was worried you wouldn't be able to do it, but I know now, if you're reading this I've met my end. Which means I want to say one thing to you—I'm proud of you, Son. I always have been. And I need you to know you've always made me proud to be your father.

Look after your family.

Dad

I'M NOT SURE WHAT TO FEEL. BUT I KNOW I HAVE TO do something. Pushing from my chair, I take both bears, and I make my way out to where my children are playing. It's time for me to sit down, and tell them a story about a king and his two princes.

. . .

THE END

If you want more from the Black Hollow Isle world, join me on Ream for a special surprise! Coming October 2023!
https://reamstories.com/danirenewrites

Are you ready for another dark, why choose romance? Then you should dive right in to Vengeance of the Fallen?

Keep reading for a snippet, or order it now only on Amazon and find it in Kindle Unlimited!

SNEAK PEEK - VENGEANCE OF THE FALLEN

CROW

Nobody starts their life out as a killer.

No child wakes up one morning and announces he's going to become a hitman.

But that's where life has brought me. It's in the eyes of my brothers in arms I find my humanity. If you can even call it that.

We've all three witnessed atrocities, and when we watched these violent acts unfolding, it wasn't on a television screen, it was real life. Perhaps it's why my mind broke. I'm certain it's why Falcon and Hawk, my brothers by all standards that matter, hunger for the same revenge that I need.

We may not be blood, but we're family all the same.

They are the only people I trust with my life.

Because they know how precious it is. Being alive, it's a gift, one that can be taken at any moment. It has brought us to the work we do. We know how to steal those last moments of someone's light and snuff it out as if they'd never existed.

Most people who know us, fear us—and they should.

We can empty your bank account, find every dark, sordid secret you've ever had hidden away, and we'll do it so we can get our payday. When your life is gone, there is no getting it back. Most times, we don't have to kill those we're hired to because once we're done they want to die anyway.

It makes our lives much easier.

Wealthy people hire us to do their dirty work, and I don't mind. I like to get my hands filthy. There's honesty in what I do. With a swipe of my blade, with the pull of a trigger, I can take out anyone who stands in my way.

There is only one person who I haven't killed yet, and it's not for the lack of trying. He's locked up tight in prison. I know he'll get out; he has connections. One day, and I know the day will come, I'll look him in the eye and watch the life drain from his face.

I want to bathe in his blood. It will be sweet vengeance.

In the darkness of the living room, I move to the balcony with a cigarette pressed between my lips. Outside, I flick the lighter and take a long, deep inhale. It's as if I can *see* the smoke curling around my nerves, collecting in my lungs, and when I breathe it out, it billows like a cloud.

The apartment is draped in darkness, and I blend into my surroundings, dressed all in black as I stand guard. My watchful gaze is trained on the building across from me. I can see her moving around her flat. She's oblivious to me. But she'll soon learn danger lurks in the shadows.

Each night I come to the apartment we bought in the city only to watch her. This is our ticket to the one thing we've been wanting for years. At first, Falcon was concerned about my plan, but when I told him she's the spawn of the most evil man we'd ever come across, he agreed.

I kept her a secret for months before I told my brothers. Something I have never done before. They know everything there is to know about me. I can't explain it, but there is something about her I want to keep to myself. A piece of her which calls to me.

A pretty little blonde with angel eyes and pouty

lips. Her body is sinful. Perhaps it's the reason why I didn't tell my brothers. Because I know the moment Falcon sees her, he'll want to enjoy every curve.

My blood heats as she moves to the second bedroom of her apartment where she'll log into her computer, touch herself, and come. Her orgasm will be real, and she'll slowly come down from her high. But deep down the guilt will eat away at her like it does every time she does it. I watch the way she rushes from the room afterward. It happens at least twice a week. She'll run to the main bedroom, cover herself in a robe, and curl up on a chair by the window as tears streak her cheeks.

Our Goldilocks is broken in ways I didn't fathom. I had no idea what was going on the first few times it happened. It doesn't stop my need to make her pay. Even if she begs for her life, she owes me one back. And I intend on taking.

I know who she really is.

I know what she did.

Meet The Fallen today!

Dani is a *USA Today* Bestselling Author of seductive and deviant romance.

Her books range from the dark to emotional, but every hero is alpha, and each heroine is strong-willed, bringing the men down to their knees.

She now lives in the UK, after moving from Cape Town, exploring cemeteries and old buildings while plotting her next book.

When she's not writing, she can be found binge-watching the latest TV series, or working on graphic design. She has a healthy addiction to reading, tattoos, coffee, and ice cream.

www.danirene.com
info@danirene.com
Spotify

www.ingramcontent.com/pod-product-compliance
Lightning Source LLC
Chambersburg PA
CBHW030805210726

48290CB00002B/442